HEAR

A NOVEL

Jacqueline Abelson

To the two most important people in my life:

Nella and Michael Abelson.

The best parents a child could ask for.

TABLE OF CONTENTS

"I was born with music inside me. Music was one of my parts. Like my ribs, my kidneys, my liver, my heart. Like my blood. It was a force already within me when I arrived on the scene. It was a necessity for me—like food or water."

– Ray Charles

PROLOGUE

My eyes open to a blinding white light.

I fall back asleep.

My eyes open to a blinding white light.

I think they're only florescent lights.

I fall back asleep.

My eyes open to a blinding white light.

I think they're only florescent lights.

God, why is this bed so lumpy?

Seriously, if you're gonna make a hospital patient happy, at least make the effort to ensure that they're comfortable in their own bed.

Wait a minute.

Skull, sore.

Tube, connected to wrist.

Scary jagged lines, moving across a screen.

This is the hospital, right?

No, it can't be.

Regular hospitals have a machine that makes that annoying *beeping* noise.

How come this one isn't making a sound?

Does this mean I'm *not* alive?

Well, if this is Heaven, it kind of sucks.

Okay, well, the lines on the machine are doing that thing that goes up and down, so maybe I'm not dead.

At least I don't think I am.

Maybe the volume is busted.

Reaching to touch machine.

Nope, no volume button there.

Work!

I hit it.

Nothing.

Go on, work!

I punch it.

Alright, I'm about to take another swing at the sucker, when I see my iPod on the dresser.

Oh God.

I remember now!

Grabbing iPod.

Selecting the first song.

Pressing play.

Putting the earphones in.

. . .

Silence.

No! No! No!

Yanking headphones out.

Grabbing the pole of the machine.

Feeling the sudden vibrations of the beeping monitor.

"MAKE A NOISE!"

Sound, not coming from my mouth.

Screaming.

Screaming to hear anything, something!

Door opens, Dr. Days is hustling in.

Mom follows closely behind, then Dad.

Um, hello?

Mom, don't cry.

Okay, now you're hugging me a little bit too tight.

Hi, Dr. Days.

What are you saying to Dad?

Your lips are moving, but I

Oh, Mom, you're talking too.

What are you and Dr. Days talking about?

Both of your lips are moving too fast.

I don't understand.

Help me.

Help me!

I feel a little dizzy.

I need sleep.

I'm tired.

I close my eyes, but I hear the voices in my head.

They're calling to be heard.

They're all speaking to me at once.

I recognize them.

I hear them.

1

I am not a big fan of religion.

If you believe in God, great. If you don't believe in God, that's great too. I seriously have better things to worry about.

Sure, God is part of my life, but I try not to think about Him (or Her). That's if you're the type of person who believes that deities should have genders. When I do think about God, I remember I hate him. Now that I think about it, he might have hated me first.

Why else would he make me skinny with absolutely no chest to speak of? He gave me hair the color of straw, and dark constellation-like freckles, which at age seventeen is no longer cute.

And, oh yeah, black tumors. Small, black rock-like bubbles.

I guess God wasn't in an artistic mood when He decided what color my tumors should be. He could've made them electric blue to match my eyes, the only feature I actually like. Must have been an oversight.

My parents try to make my life normal. Yet it's a tad bit hard to call your household normal if both of your parents are convinced that the new freckle on your left arm is a growing tumor. This then results in my ass being dragged to the hospital, where – more often than not – after hours in some ER with flickering neon lights and outdated *People* magazines, some doctor pokes and prods me, before alleviating my parents' concerns.

"Thank God it was just skin irritation," Dad would hide his nervous laugh whenever we drove home after a false alarm.

Yeah. *Thank God.*

It wasn't until I was a sophomore in high school that doctors gave a name to my disease: *Neurofibromatosis* Type II. A scary name for something that causes tumors to grow along the nervous system. The tumors scatter themselves into clusters. In my case, they mostly drip down the front of my chest to the back of my legs.

When I turned thirteen, Dad taught me about genetics. A few days later, I could solve and understand the purpose of a Punnett Square. It also didn't take long for me to figure out I was screwed.

I remember this one time in eighth grade; I was sitting at the kitchen table reviewing all the basic materials about chromosomes and mutated genes from my science textbook. My entire right leg was mummified by a white bandage to remove the tumors I'd gotten from the hospital only two days earlier. Well, thanks to my easily distracted mind-set, I was more interested in how many kids I could get to sign the bandages on my arm than remembering that I had a science test the next morning. So, genius here forgot her review sheet at school, and when she realized that her review sheet was sitting on top of her math textbook in her locker, she screamed. Instantly, Mom slammed down the stairs in her tennis shoes and into the dining room.

She found me with my mouth hanging open and my eyes wide in shock. I stomped on my bandaged leg and threw my arms into the air, while staring down at my science book. "What? What? What is it, Charlotte?" Mom rushed to the table. "Did you find another tumor? Where is it? Charlotte, where is it? Marc!" she called Dad. "Marc, get down here!"

I heard Dad, in his penny loafers, rushing down the stairs.

"Isabel! Charlotte! Where's the tumor?" his eyes blazed from behind his black-rimmed glasses.

"I forgot it!" I cried.

"You forgot where you saw the tumor?" Mom's breath quickened as if each inhalation would keep me alive, instead of her.

I'm also on the slow side to realize my surroundings. I looked into the face of my panic-stricken father, noticed the car keys clutched in one hand and his other hand gripping the handle to the door.

Once I had explained to them my stupidity of misplacing my review sheet, their shoulders relaxed.

"Okay," Mom then answered slowly. "But does anything hurt?"

I want to be clear, this is a typical scene at my house. I mean, I always appreciate the fact that my parents care so much about me, but there is no "normal" in my house. No normal cursing, crying, confusion or anger. Every little hiccup puts my parents into some sort of lock-down mode.

2

If I wanted to sue God, how would I do it?

I would probably need to ask my dad, considering that this is his profession.

Do I need a lawyer?

Does God have attorneys?

Do they wear expensive suits?

My argument would probably go down like this: "Ladies and gentlemen of the jury: this case involves a promise, a broken contract between my client, Charlotte Goode, and the Defendant. The Defendant claims we are created in His own image, does He not? Imagine this. A real estate agent shows you a beautiful house, and you buy it, but when you move in, you discover that the house is infested with rats. Do you just accept things the way they are? Or do you hold someone accountable? A body is just like a home. It's a home to your soul. And God is the real estate agent. So when Mr. and Mrs. Goode brought their beautiful daughter Charlotte into this world, they expected God to honor His agreement to create their daughter in His image. They did not expect that their daughter's "home" would be infested with a rare genetic disease.

"This is not the house Charlotte was promised."

Case closed.

I remember that day so vaguely.

I was pulled from the middle of my sixth grade class because Miss Greene found me whimpering in the corner of her classroom and cradling my arm, which was spotted with tumors. *This is all a misunderstanding,* I remember thinking when my parents took me to the hospital. *Dr. Days will change her mind once she sees my charts. She'll then tell me that it was all a big mistake. This nightmare isn't mine. It belongs to the girl in the bed next to me. She has cancer. Look at me, I'm twelve years old, a sixth grader who has her future laid out before her. Middle school, high school, her first boyfriend, her first job, fame as a violinist. A bridesmaid at her sister's wedding, an aunt for her firstborn. Come on! It isn't fair!*

There was an eerie silence as I waited those painful moments for Dr. Days to return and correct her diagnosis.

But she never came back.

3

Ice skates for ostriches.

French fries dipped in chocolate milkshakes.

Spraying whipped cream into my mouth from the can.

SpongeBob.

Commercials for the Shamwow product.

This is just a slice of what circles through my head 24/7 when I'm not thinking about cancer or other things that make my life a bit suckish.

They are also the things that I share with my best friend, Lexi Abbott.

It's the evening after our first day of junior year. What better way to celebrate being one grade above the rest than prank-calling the new freshman class to see if they are willing to donate one dollar to the Ice Skates for Ostriches Foundation?

"Yes, is this Reba Fest?" I say in a low, masculine tone.

Lexi and I stop at Burger Lounge on Orange Avenue for milk-shakes and fries before starting. We pull our ice skates for ostriches prank on the first name we see on the new high school roster.

As always, Lexi sits across from me, her black, braided hair draped over her right shoulder, dipping her salty fries into the thick liquid of her shake. She bites down on her tongue to stave off her laughter (and a rapid end to our afternoon's entertainment).

"Um . . . yes," said an uncertain, young voice on the other end.

"This is Henry William calling to inform you about an epidemic that has hit one of our beloved animals. You may not know this but the ostrich is going extinct. So here at Ice Skates for Ostriches, we are trying to save the ostrich population by tying ice skates to their feet so that they can glide across frozen lakes or rivers away from any predators. All it takes is one dollar to save their species."

Lexi lets out an amused snort as her head collapses onto the table, muffling the loud laughter with her hands.

"Is this a joke?" Reba Fest asks quizzically.

"Miss, this is too serious a matter to joke about."

Lexi slowly raises her head up to me, her eyes curious as to what card I'm playing next on the poor, gullible Reba.

"No, no, Sir. It's just I've never heard of this kind of situation before. I didn't even know that the ostriches were going extinct."

"Sit . . . situation?" I pretend to sound insulted. "Miss, do you think that this is just a 'situation?' It's a matter of life and death for these poor birds. Don't you want to see them gliding beautifully along the frozen rivers of Africa away from any jaguars or leopards? Or do you want to see them pounced upon and have their pretty necks ripped from their bodies?"

"Alright, alright, alright," Reba Fest squeaks.

Lexi throws a fistful of fries into her mouth to silence the near fever pitch of giggles.

"Alright?" I ask curiously, raising one of my eyebrows.

"Yeah, yeah, a dollar right? Who do I send it to?"

"Oh you know. Make out a letter to The Ice Skates for Ostriches Foundation. P.O. Box 123 Poor Schmuck Avenue, Antarctica, 10001."

And I snap my phone closed.

Tears roll down Lexi's face as we laugh harder than I think we've laughed in our lives. People are looking at us from other tables, and I don't care. It's junior year. I'm in remission and I'm with my best friend.

After our meal, Lexi and I walk together to my house, where I break open the seal to the new can of Reddi-whip in my fridge. We throw ourselves onto the couch and spray coils of the white whipped cream into our open mouths, as an episode of *SpongeBob Squarepants* plays on the TV. When the episode goes to commercial, the Shamwow guy appears! Lexi jokes that since Mr. Shamwow Guy is such a good pitchman, he might be able to sell our Ice Skates for Ostriches Foundation to everyone on Coronado.

I better keep that in mind.

4

I can't hear my own thoughts. Only the notes.

People are stopping and going before the door to the music wing to listen to my violin. I find this normal, because this has been going on since the fourth grade. There are only three schools on the island of Coronado: Coronado Elementary School, Coronado Middle School and finally Coronado High School. Unfortunately, there's no Coronado College since the island, along the San Diego coastline, is so tiny. Yet, we have managed to establish a Naval Air Base up in North Beach. Why do we need a Naval Air Base on such a dinky island? Nobody knows and nobody really cares, if you want my answer.

Currently, I am only 1 out of the 115 students enrolled in Coronado High School.

We're the type of school that no one outside of Coronado knows about because our school ad does not appear in the *San Diego Outlook* like the other big-name schools in Carlsbad or La Jolla. But on the island, our school gets written up a lot. The only problem is that no one reads *The Coronado Crown News* because it's likely that your neighbor knows more about who went sailing this morning at Coronado Cays or ate at Alexander's Pizza than any reporter would ever know.

But our school is just like any normal school. Although it's a bit hard to call your school normal if your math teacher lives in a 5.1 radius near your home and you carpool to school with your history teacher. Furthermore, 50 percent of the time you are likely to know almost everyone on Coronado Island, while the remaining 50 percent are people you've never heard of because they go to school off the island but live on Coronado.

We do get a lot of free time though. I have a study block as my last class of the day, and I spend it in the music wing of the school, playing my violin.

Sometimes, I am there alone, which I find better, since the silence makes the music sound more real to me. There are very few interruptions as I hear the bow against the wired strings of the violin. Horsehair and wires. How can those two things come together to create something as beautiful as this?

Now I'm just getting ahead of myself.

I don't normally act like this. You know, serene and tranquil.

I'm more loud and obnoxious, according to Lexi. But sometimes I can't tell if she's being cynical or honest.

There is a tap on the door.

"What?" I look up.

It's Lexi, her chocolate brown eyes staring at me.

"Sounds good," she says, leaning against the doorframe.

"Do you need a ride home or are you walking to your dad's studio?" I ask, ignoring her compliment. I've heard it a million times.

"I'm walking." Lexi folds her lips, her signature annoyed expression. "I don't really want to go, but Dad says it's important."

"Oh *really?*"

The bell rings, signaling the end of the period and the end of the school day. A throng of people flood the hallway. The sound of lockers squeaking open and slamming close echo loudly, as Lexi continues to lean against the doorframe to the room.

"Last week this band came in to record a song and they were such jerks. They're coming back today to lay down some more tracks." Lexi rolls her eyes as she speaks.

"Hang in there, Lexi," I encourage her with a smile as I pick up my violin case and tuck my violin and bow inside. "Next time, you tell them who's boss, and if they still don't respect you, I'll drive down and kick their asses."

I stop in the business district of Coronado and park my black Toyota in the reserved space for *Musique Magazine* employees. I enter the elevator that takes me up to the third floor. The receptionist, Mage, notices me without taking her eyes off the computer screen behind her desk. "Miss Gaukler wants to see you in her office."

Ugh . . . I think, trying to keep it light. *She probably wants me to run down to Starbucks to get her mint-mocha-chip-frappuccino-blended-coffee-with chocolate-whipped cream.*

I still can't wrap my head around the fact that my boss, Mel Gaukler, is stuck on this tiny island, which has no big music scene to speak of. She had become known for her work in the '70s, by reporting on bands from Led Zeppelin and David Bowie to the *San Diego Outlook.* She doesn't like to admit it, but everyone in the office suspects that at one time Mel was a groupie who followed the bands whenever they visited the SoCal area. Then, after years of being straightened out in journalism school (and maybe a one-time stop to rehab) she obtained a position in the early '90s at the *Los Angeles Times*. She left in 1998 when she started the monthly *Musique Magazine* on Coronado Island. Even when my parents hooked me up as a paid intern for Mel, the magazine was pretty much independent. I give Mel credit though, for maintaining order in her business without a big-name publishing company as a companion. Still, she runs the place like it's *Billboard* magazine in Manhattan. But as long as Mel is selling 16,000 copies monthly with my music reviews printed on page 22, then we're both happy.

"Ah, Charlotte, you're here," Mel pushes back a strand of brown hair from the bun that she has tied up on her head.

Mel still has her head in her paperwork but starts talking anyway. Nobody here is big on eye contact.

"I have a question for you." She talks to the paper on her desk, which is decorated with red edits from her pen. "Do you remember how much money we collected from the benefit we threw for cancer last year?"

Whenever Mel asks a question, you feel like you're on a game show. Answer her question correctly and she might – just might – smile at you, which is worth much more than the cash you would hypothetically win. I say this with the most upmost respect for Mel, even though she makes me run to Starbucks to order her ridiculously named caffeinated drink.

She does this because she knows that I'm easy to annoy.

"Roughly $58,000?" It's a guess, but according to Mel's email announcement last year, she stated that we *almost* made $60,000 from our cancer benefit.

Once every year, Mel puts on a live show by selecting one local band around the Coronado area for a cover shoot and a five-page spread. Each member of the winning band collects $5,000 to play at the magazine's benefit to raise money for whatever illness makes the most public headline. And of course, the magazine pays for the band to go on tour around the San Diego area.

"*Roughly*," Mel reiterates. "The money doesn't come out of nowhere, yet we've never broken the $60,000 barrier."

"Well, have you decided on the theme for this year's benefit?" I hinted.

"If you're hoping that I'm going out of my way to promote your neuro-disease, you are sadly mistaken," Mel says.

"Darn, I was hoping to get $60,000 out of you."

This was one of the first things that I had to come clean with to Mel when I began working for her. Because I check in regularly with my doctor at least twice a month for X-ray scans, I miss a lot of work days. After all, Dr. Days takes her sweet time, making sure that no tumors are popping up inside and outside of my body. I mean, just yesterday, I missed Lucy Wake's goodbye party at the office because I went in to get a MRI and a blood test. However, Dr. Days was chatting for ten minutes to the nurse who was suppose to draw my blood. I only wanted to get this done and over with, but Doc apparently thought that it was more important to ask Nurse Penny if Dante and Lulu would ever get together on *General Hospital* than getting my blood drawn for medical purposes.

"Hate to disappoint you, but multiple sclerosis beat you to the punch." Mel finally looks up at me. "And that's why I need you."

"Me?"

"Sit."

I sit in the cushioned chair, as Mel clicks her pen and leans forward in her seat.

"Because Lucy is now gone, she will no longer reside as our band selector this year. During her final days in the office, she only completed half of the assignment that I gave her." She reaches for her desk drawer and pulls out a black folder.

"From the dozens of bands I've asked her to evaluate on Coronado, she narrowed her selection down to just two: Bond Boys and Lennox. The MS benefit is next month and only one of these bands can play." She holds out the folder to me. "I'm assigning you to finish Lucy's job by picking one of these two bands."

Surprised, I take Mel's folder and open it, scanning the names, dates and instruments that each of the band members play.

"Mage wrote out a schedule of where to meet them, what day and what time."

"This is such a kind offer . . ."

"Don't flatter yourself," Mel rolls her eyes at me. "I only picked you because you have a great ear when it comes to music. So far, your album reviews are spot on, very detailed. I needed someone who has a good relationship to music, just as Lucy did."

"Right, then." I smile at her.

Back in the elevator, I wait for the doors to slide closed. Once I'm in the parking lot, I begin punching my fists in the air.

5

The next morning, my parents get a call from Dr. Days, requesting our presence.

An hour later, I'm sitting between my parents in Dr. Days' office, which, may I add, isn't exactly the most pleasant place to be if you live on an island. Sure, there are portraits of the beach and the sea along the walls to give the visitors a sense of tranquility, but it doesn't change the fact that you are in your oncologist's office. Which can only mean bad news. In fact, I believe there's some conspiracy that oncologists only hire certain interior decorators to make the office seem less depressing. Seriously, would you rather have the news of your stomach cancer be revealed to you in a dark dungeon, or would you rather have the news delivered in a room with calm periwinkle wallpaper, and fashion magazines of beautiful people fanned out on the table?

But no one wants news like that. Yet, in the real world, the truth is only delivered to you through falsely cheery pretenses, like that fake—but almost real—fern in the back of the office.

I pick up a copy of *Vogue,* or is it *Vanity Fair*? What's the difference? They're both 90 percent ads, while the remaining 10 percent is actual intellectual writing. But I flip though the glossy pages and pretend to be interested in an article about weight loss.

I can't help but think about my older sister, Rose. I wonder how much weight she will lose after giving birth?

Dr. Days enters and greets us, holding a thick brown folder in one hand as she brushes away the bangs of her red hair.

Ever since I met Dr. Days, and even up to this day, I've never actually gotten used to her name.

Dr. *Days.*

As in, Dr. "you - only - have - two - days - to - live."

The uneasiness in her name, especially for someone who is an oncologist, has always made me nervous. Surgery is not a new thing for me. In the past, whenever I went in to get a tumor removed from my body, Dr. Days was always the one who would operate on me. Before an operation, she would try to be all jocular and chipper with me. All smiling with her ginger hair tied back into a ponytail like some ignorant schoolgirl she'd say, "You've had quite a week, Charlotte. But not to worry, we'll fix you up in a jiffy." But I bet she secretly knows how many days I have left until I croak.

"Alright, I apologize for calling you in this early," Dr. Days says, walking to the light box over her desk and opening the folder. "But yesterday, our technician at the MRI spotted something unusual in one of your X-rays."

Dr. Days slips an X-ray under the clips of the rectangular light panel.

My brain looked like a thick U-shaped steak bone. On both sides, puzzled in-between the crevices of my brain, are two small gray blotches in the shape of a lumpy, upside-down heart.

At this point, the gray and black scan seems out of place. It doesn't match the serene blue paintings on the walls or the polished wood of Dr. Days' desk. It was like playing that game where you look for mismatched items.

I can see Dad's face morphing to a pale shade and Mom's chest rising and falling rapidly under her cardigan.

"Charlotte, this is important, so please listen." Dr. Days takes a pen from her lab coat pocket and points to the X-ray.

"The scan shows two acoustic neuroma tumors pressing against your brainstem. However, even though these tumors are benign, it's particularly troublesome because it's impacting both of your auditory nerves," Dr. Days says. "Obviously, the tumors have to come out."

No shit, Sherlock, I think.

You would assume, that after six years of going under the knife to remove tumor after tumor, that I would be use, to being sedated, cut open and operated on. Because obviously, that's every young girl's fantasy. Sometimes I even think that the game Operation is based on me. But frankly, it really annoys the hell out of me. Being all drugged up on morphine, being poked and prodded like I'm some sort of bacteria in a Petri dish and–worst of all–wearing that ridiculous open-backed hospital gown that feels like tissue paper against my skin.

"Okay," I huff, clearly not delighted that I have to wear the gown again. "So when would I have to go in for the . . ." My voice trails off.

The meaning of the words finally hit me. I've had tumors appear on my arms, legs, stomach and chest. All of which were easily operated on and removed.

BUT HOLY SHIT! How the hell did two tumors appear in my brain?! How long have they been there growing or manifesting? Why haven't I felt it before? Maybe I have. Maybe from all the headaches I've simply ignored. But goddamnit! How the hell was I suppose to know that a tiny headache was actually a tumor?! This wasn't a simple, "let's quickly get you into surgery," speed run. No. It was *fucking* brain surgery! The scariest surgery on the face of the planet, next to open-heart surgery!

I feel like unzipping my body and crawling away from Dr. Days' somber blue eyes.

"We would have to operate on you as soon as possible," Dr. Days says to me. "However, there is something else we need to discuss." She pulls out her chair and takes a seat at her desk, looking directly at me. "It is a virtual certainty that no matter how we attack this problem, Charlotte, you *will* lose your hearing."

This is a bad joke, right? I agree something is wrong with my "auditory nerves" because it sounds like Dr. Days has just said I'm going to be deaf. But the room is absolutely still, as everything shrinks down around that one phrase: "Lose your hearing."

But proof that I'm not deaf yet, I hear a tiny cry escapes from my mom's throat, and I see the sudden tears rolling down her cheeks. Dad sits in his seat; the news has made him motionless.

"W-what will ha-happen to h-her?" Mom's voice quivers with shaky sobs.

"Well, because the tumors are growing from the brainstem, it will press on the brain's ventricular system, leading to an abnormal accumulation of cerebrospinal fluid in the ventricles of the brain. This can cause seizures or even a potential fatal consequence." Her voice is reassuring and calm. She might as well say: "Hey Charlotte, you better get ready, cuz you're gonna die soon." But no. The unfazed tone in her voice seems like she is used to delivering bad news to patients every day. I begin to wonder if they teach you how to pull off the ultimate poker face in medical school.

"So what you're saying is that she'll die if she waits too long on the surgery?" My lawyer dad emphases our new reality. I feel him reaching for my hand and the instant squeeze of his fingers against my scarred skin.

"If we can schedule immediate surgery for her, she won't face a fatal outcome."

"But she would have to give up her hearing." Dad's grip on my hand fastens.

"By the size of the tumors," Dr. Days says, pointing to the X-ray, "now's the time to go in. In a couple of months, they'll simply be too big to operate on safely."

So it all comes down to hearing or life?

"What happens next?" Dad says as he swallows.

"We should start scheduling the surgery. We can begin as early as Monday morning."

"Wait. Monday morning?" I hear my own voice faintly escaping through my lips. "That's in three days."

Three days.

"How big can these tumors actually get? They're not malignant or anything, so what's the rush?"

Dr. Days taps her pen against her desk, generating the right words to balance the dreadful news.

"These are not the normal tumors you are use to witnessing. Because of their rapid growth, they threaten to intervene with the brain's normal system. As the tumors grow larger and larger you're at risk of seizures. Right now the tumors are the size of half-dollar coins."

Dr. Days continues to speak, but I don't take in her words. I close off her voice as a white-hot pang attacks the center of my chest. I avoid Dr. Days' eyes and look behind her to her wall of pride. Brown University for undergrad and Harvard for medical school. Board certifications and professional awards and commendations.

I do not see these plaques as symbols of knowledge. Instead, I feel like these framed diplomas are mocking me. The degrees may signify Dr. Days' understanding of medicine, but her degrees don't know how much I rely on my hearing. They don't know that my favorite part of entering an ice cream parlor is listening to the jingle of the bell over the door. They don't even know that my preferred note on a music sheet is middle C. These degrees are just rectangular sheets of paper with words scribbled on them. There is no emotional connection; and the longer I stare at the framed documents on the wall, the angrier I become.

"We'll need some more scans and a blood test—" Dr. Days' voice returns. I let go of my dad's hand and quickly sit up in my seat.

"No! You just told me I have two, TWO, goddamn tumors lodged in my head!" I shout. "Now you *propose* that I just count down the days before every sound on this planet disappears!" The back of my skull is throbbing, and I can't tell if it's my anger for Dr. Days or the tumors behind my ears. "Do you even know how important my hearing is?" I spear my finger at Dr. Days.

My mind is boiling, battling between anger and fear. I am waiting to see who will win. So far anger has control over the battlefield of my conscious. "I play the violin! I have a job as a music critic at a magazine! I want to go to Juilliard for college! I want to be a musician when I grow up, Dr. Days! Doesn't that matter too?"

Shaking as I point my finger at my helpless oncologist, I feel the wet uncoiled ribbon of tears roll down my face. "Don't my own opinions count?"

Fear is now taking over.

The faces of my parents and Dr. Days suddenly lose all their features. They are nothing more than blank ovals with hair—looking at me in desperation.

I'm aware of a heavy noise, and realize it's me, gasping for air.

Convinced that this room with the periwinkle wallpaper is sucking the air from out of my lungs, I run out of Dr. Days' office and make it to the hallway.

Once away from Dr. Days' prying eyes, I lean my back against the wall and sink to the floor.

A few minutes later, the door to the office swings open and Dad steps out. There is no expression in his eyes behind his square glasses.

He doesn't speak as he walks over and sits himself next to me on the floor. I am staring at my hands and sniffling as Dad's arms come up to wrap me close to his chest.

Immediately, I slip back into tears. We sit in silence for a while before Dad's voice returns to my ears. "A month," he says. "Dr. Days will let you keep your hearing for a month."

TUESDAY / WEDNESDAY

It feels like forever since I've heard a sound.

Maybe it has been forever.

I don't remember the last time I picked up my violin, or played a note. I can't even recall what my voice sounds like anymore.

But ever since I began drifting in and out of consciousness, I've been able to feel my heart beating, but not hear its rhythm.

Everything else in my body seems to be working properly.

Smell: Almonds and ethanol.

Taste: Like I have alcohol in my mouth whenever I swallow.

Sight: Light coming from window.

Touch: Itchy bed sheets, and that damn hospital gown!

Sound: . . .

Can't say much about that.

I'm exhausted and will even admit, a tiny bit delirious.

I am aware of the heavy, dull headache and acute pain behind both of my ears.

For several seconds, I remember a fragment of sound, before I return to the silence in my room.

I wonder where my parents are.

I haven't seen them since I woke up.

Oh, Nurse Frizzy is here! Come to check-up on me, have you?

How can I not call you Frizzy, when you're an old nurse with kinky blond hair?

Yeah, yeah, I see your mouth is moving—

Oh, now you're using your hands.

Palm is facing up.

Fingers loose and free from tension.

Oh, I wasn't aware that you were trained in the art of sign language.

Are you ready for your morning treatment?

Gee, Dr. Days thinks of everything for me.

I sign back, *Whatever.*

Frizzy comes around to my bed, pops a disposable cone on a otoscope, sticks it into both of my ears.

Throws the cone away.

Brings around the blood pressure cuff.

Inflates the device.

Tears the cuff off.

Writes something down on my charts.

Smiles.

Signs to me, *I'll be back.*

Returns a few minutes later with my breakfast tray of jello and a lump that looks like mashed potatoes.

Frizzy leaves.

I don't see her for the rest of the day.

My parents come by to see me, crying and repeatedly kissing my face.

I reach for both of them and try to squeeze, but my entire body aches when I lift up my arms for a hug.

Mom: Signing something that I can't really understand.

I sit in silence.

I don't respond.

Dad: Signing something that I also can't understand.

I'm not going to lie.

They're doing a pretty awful job at trying to communicate with me.

Yet, I know they're trying.

They're really trying their best.

I raise my hand and give them a thumbs up.

It's the only gesture all of us can understand.

Mom's smile is weak and Dad slowly nods his head.

Oh, Frizzy, you're back!

Ah, saying something to my parents in that language I no longer can hear.

Oh, okay, Mom and Dad are getting up to leave.

They don't let your family stay with you 24/7 because it's some infection risk or something.

Bye, Mom.

Bye, Dad.

How long has it been now?

Two days?

Three days?

A week?

Jesus Christ!

How long does it take me to recover?

Oh, Frizzy just signed to me that she's going to get me out of this room.

Wheelchair time!

Damnit!

Will this headache ever go away?

I'll have to ask if Frizzy will give me an extra dose of painkillers.

Lately, she's been holding back on the morphine.

Wheelchairs are fun.

I wish I could use my legs though.

I haven't felt them since my operation.

I'm beginning to wonder if they even still work.

Wheeling out the room.

Wheeling down the hall.

Someone's door is open.

Wrinkled face old man on a ventilator. Eyes seem half-dead. Grandpa Death.

Rolling by another open door.

Bald kid with an IV. Cancer. I can relate. Cancer Kid.

One other door.

Girl whose arm is in a cast. That's what you get when you fall out of a tree, kid. Cast Chick.

Wheeling into the elevator.

Doors close.

Doors open.

Ooo . . . we're in the cafeteria.

Feeling my stomach tingle with hunger.

Frizzy signs to me, asking what I want for breakfast, before parking me at an empty table next to the window.

It's a beautiful day.

Sun streaming down between puffy clouds.

I see the ocean in the distance, the blue water radiating.

Are the birds singing today?

Are the waves crashing down against the shore?

Frizzy returns with my plate of hash browns and bacon.

I pick up my silverware and begin eating.

I chew. I swallow.

I chew. I swallow.

I stop.

There is something missing.

There is no silverware against silverware.

No knives against forks.

No forks against knives.

I look at the cluster of patients in the cafeteria.

As the patients cut their pancakes and spear their sausages, do they not hear the sounds that each of their utensils make?

Do they not appreciate the symphony of china against metal?

The clattering of the spoon against the empty bowl of cereal?

Before the tumors, before Dr. Days informed me about my judgment day, I wouldn't have even noticed the sounds my silverware made whenever I ate a meal.

But watching everyone eat, and hearing no sounds where there should be sounds, is suddenly distracting.

I drop the silverware on my plate.

Frizzy!

Where's Frizzy?!

There you are, sashaying and smiling over to me like everything is okay.

I open my mouth.

"I want to leave."

Frizzy? Frizzy, your smile is gone.

Why are you looking at me like that?

Do you not understand what I just said?

It's plain English, I'll say it again.

"I want to leave."

Frizzy, why are you just staring at me?

Fuck, have I gone mute too?

Maybe I have.

I can't hear my own voice.

My melodramatic voice that I used to take so much pride in.

"Please." I say. "I don't want to be here anymore."

I'm being pulled backward, away from the table.

Frizzy is guiding me back toward the elevator.

My voice . . .

I suddenly realize.

My voice. My voice. My voice.

The doors close, and I think, *I will never be heard again.*

6

A pole impaling my chest while walking next to a construction site.

A car accident splitting me into two.

Falling down a flight of stairs.

Getting shot.

Drowning in a pool.

If I had to pick my own death, it wouldn't be a tumor that would end my life.

The French had a cool way of terminating someone's life.

How does death by guillotine sound?

The next day I get off the elevator and march through *Musique Magazine's* waiting room.

Mage says something, but I don't hear her.

Probably about Mel being on a conference call or something.

But my feet carry me straight toward Mel's office, grasping the black folder in my sweaty hands.

I reach Mel's office and storm in without a knock.

Some people consider this rude. I say this is important.

Mel's black eyes snap up at me while she balances her phone between her ear and shoulder.

I drop the black folder onto her desk.

It sounds like a slap in the face.

"I can't do it."

A gap of silence expands between us.

"I'll call you back," says Mel as she puts the phone down and looks up at me.

"Well, that is a wonderful act. Barging in while I'm in the middle of an important meeting with our sponsors. Must be serious, or at least it better be serious," she says, annoyed.

"I'm so sorry, Mel," I rush, "I've been working on what I want to say to you for hours, but now you'll have to forgive me because I don't quite know where to begin."

"Well, how about you start by telling me why you can't do this anymore?" She holds the black folder up.

I open my mouth, but instead of words a sob comes out. Before I know it, the floodgates open. I explain to her about my visit to Dr. Days' office. I tell her about the tumors.

Never have I had a tumor grow on my brain before! Let alone two!

Oh God! Will it hurt while it grows? Will it cause any more damage to my other nerves?

And brain surgery! Someone is going to slice open my head!

My head!

But I have to go deaf. I need to go deaf to save my life.

But why? Why my hearing? What will I do when I'm deaf?

I can't talk on the phone, I can't go to Juilliard, I can't play my violin . . . I won't be able to talk to Lexi anymore! Or hear Squidward Tentacles on *SpongeBob Squarepants* play his clarinet at an elementary level. That is always my favorite part, listening to Squidward's frequently missed notes whenever he plays his clarinet!

No more blasting the music from in my car.

No more *Musique Magazine*!

My mouth keeps moving.

Why can't I stop?

I fight back a swell of tears.

The color drains from Mel's face.

She purses her lips together.

I tell her, while a bubble of saliva rises in my throat, that I love this magazine and because of this magazine I love music.

Mel is quiet.

Silence is deafening.

Okay, that's not funny . . .

I violently blow into the tissue Mel hands me, and I accept the small cup of coffee Mage hands me before excusing herself from Mel's office.

I take a swallow of the black coffee, calming my nerves, but not my tears as they continue to fall.

God, this fucking sucks! Out of all the people in the world, here I am bawling in front of my boss. I guess it was easier said than done, when Dad told me to inform Mel of my predicament.

"I'm sorry," I mumble. "I'm sorry, sorry, sorry, Mel."

God, I must look like a fucking mess.

"I just think that maybe someone else should take on this job," I nod to the black folder on Mel's desk. "Give it to Leon Murray or Katie Wang. I can't—" my voice snags on another upcoming sob, "I can't do this."

Mel makes sure that the door to her office is closed and stands, while leaning against her desk, in front of me.

"Have I ever told you why I hired you in the first place?" Her voice is leveled instead of pragmatic this time.

I shake my head.

"Because your dad never shuts up about you." She crosses her arms over her chest. "When I started this magazine, your dad made sure that all of my credentials were in place to buy this office space. And whenever I was sued, or one of our workers was sued, your dad stepped in and did us a huge favor. And every time we left the courtroom because of some ridiculous copyright infringement, he always told me how you had an ear for music. In fact, every sentence he said to me always involved *Charlotte* and *music*."

I must have been in sixth grade when Dad began working over-time for Mel, helping her start up her business. The first time I officially met Mel, was when I was a freshman in high school, and she had wanted to read the music reviews I had begun posting on a blog. A few weeks later she hired me. I knew Dad had always been Mel's lawyer, but I never knew that he talked to her about me. I guess that's how she became more understanding of my disease.

"So when I hired you, do you know what the first thing I thought of was?"

"What?"

"I thought, 'Oh shit, why did I hire this pesky teenager to write up my reviews for this magazine?' "

I can't help it, but I laugh. Just a little though.

"And guess what? It was the best decision I ever made," Mel says. "At first I thought it was going to be 'I like this song because' dot, dot, dot. But you added depth in your reviews. You back-up your statements with logical explanations and—" she stops herself. "It's hard to explain. But your writing flows so well that you convey the message and the feeling to the reader. Which is hard for a reviewer to do."

Mel takes the black folder from her desk and holds it out to me.

"When the time comes, we'll discuss your position at this maga-zine. But you're not deaf yet, Charlotte. And I don't want Leon Murray or Katie Wang. With the days you have left of your hearing, I want *you* to finish this job."

I gaze at the black folder, a black abyss of the future that has been taken away from me.

"*When* I'm deaf," I say. "I'm not coming back, am I?"

Mel's mouth falls into a frown, "I never said that."

"Doesn't need to be said. You can't hire a music reviewer who is deaf."

"True," Mel clicks her fingers against the glossy surface of her desk. "But I can still hire someone who can voice her opinions in writing. And though writing is read, it is always heard."

She looks down at the folder, still in her hands. "Now are you going to take this, or are you going to make me wait all day for a decision? Also, go downstairs and get me some Starbucks. I haven't eaten breakfast yet."

7

After Dr. Days' explanation that the tumors in my brain are growing bigger, every headache I have makes me think that the tumors are the cause. As disturbing as it is, it at least helps focus my mind.

The next day after the grueling visit at Dr. Days' office, I sleep in for two whole hours until I hear the toaster pop out what smells like burnt toast.

I go downstairs and it is obvious from the faint smoke curling from the kitchen that someone had forgotten how long to toast the bread.

I stand in the doorway of the dining room. Mom is sitting at the table, her back facing me. She's wearing the same clothes as the day before, and her hair is up in a bird's nest. Dad's sitting next to her, and they exchange low whispers.

I hear my name repeated a couple of times, as well as the forbidden "T" word, and finally: "We need to be strong, Isabelle. For Charlotte, okay?"

"Guys?" My voice squeaks from behind the doorway.

Together, both of my parents turn around to face me.

My stomach instantly drops.

The glow from Mom's cheeks is gone, replaced by a tired pale face. As soon as I see her eyes, swollen and red from the crying I pretended not to hear last night, I have the sudden urge to fling myself into her arms and cry with her.

But I can't command my feet to move. Then Mom's eyes well up again, her hands begin to tremble, and a loud sob escapes from her lips. Her shoulders violently quiver as she draws in a breath, "Oh God, I'm so sorry Marc—" And then Dad takes her in his arms as she buries her face in his chest.

What was my mom sorry for? Sorry for having me? Sorry for not being strong enough for me? Then I figure it out: She's sorry that she couldn't do enough to protect me.

As Mom's sobs are muffled by Dad's shirt, I take a step back and sit down on the first step of the stairs.

A few minutes go by and I can still hear Mom's cries. Seeing Mom's sobbing was bad enough, listening to it was worse.

In due course, Dad got Mom to calm down. Together they go upstairs to their room and shut the door. I don't mind. My presence made Mom bawl, and Mom's drained and haunted face almost made me want to cry out too. It makes sense.

Because the three of us—Mom, Dad and I—are all infected by this plague of melancholy, I begin to wonder about my sister, whom I assume has no knowledge of my condition.

Rose and I were close when we were small. Now, I only see her four to five times a year.

She and her husband, Andrew, live in Beverly Hills. Although only two and a half hours from Coronado, she seems worlds away.

My sister is pregnant with her first child. I'm going to be an aunt. Rose announced it to my parents while I was having surgery on my thigh, so I wasn't there to witness what I can guess was my parents' first bit of joy, especially after all the surgeries that I had been through.

Rose is already seven months pregnant! The last time that I saw her was on the Fourth of July. Back then she looked as if she were going to pop like all the fireworks exploding in the sky that night.

Rose travels around designing posters promoting new television shows. I suspect that she gets paid a lot of money—not from her TV posters—but from bossing people around. I imagine she's good at it, with all the practice she got on me.

When I was seven and Rose was thirteen, all of our grandparents died. It was very strange. One died in May and the others died one right after the other. A heart attack (June). A stroke (July). A car accident (August). Poof. They were gone. I got so freaked out that I thought that *I* would die next when September came around. I refused to go to school. I retreated to my room and slept with a toy sword under my pillow to fight off anything that came to get me. I was going to be ready for Death. No easy pickings here.

Rose had the patience to calm me down. Our grandparents' deaths were just a coincidence. There was no reason to it. When my parents couldn't reach me, Rose could.

Rose is smart, and I'll admit, prettier than me. She believes she is lucky to have landed a guy like Andrew. He isn't all that attractive from the outside, but Rose loves him.

I, however, do not.

My parents, of course, adore Andrew. Dad goes running with him in the mornings whenever they stay with us, and Mom proudly calls Andrew her son. But that is just my parents.

Andrew's the kind of guy who will say two sentences to me but have an entire conversation with his BlackBerry. His father is the mayor of Santa Barbara, and he is the oldest out of three children, all of whom grew up with silver spoons extending from their mouths. He owns a bank in Beverly Hills. He doesn't work, he just owns the bank building. This leaves me to question if all those emails Andrew keeps getting from his Blackberry, were from his buddies on the polo team (that he used to brag about) or from his parents who live on a exquisite estate in Hope Ranch.

My parents and I have visited Andrew's side of the family a couple of times at their estate. It's a nice place but with snobbish people.

When Andrew is around Rose or my parents or anyone else besides me, he acts totally cool and funny; when he's stuck with me, he becomes somewhat flippant.

I never knew what his deal was with me. Is it because he is embarrassed in the presence of a seventeen-year-old girl? Or is it because three years ago at a Thanksgiving dinner with his family at their Hope Ranch estate, we had to drag everyone to the Santa Barbara Cottage Hospital because the tumors on my back began to swell?

Maybe it's that.

I take the kitchen phone from its cradle, head to the backyard and sit down on the patio. I spot a few of my raggedy shoes lined up next to the door, and I notice how the cement of the patio is littered with specks and tiny piles of sand from my last trek down to the beach. It is a cloudy day, typical SoCal weather. The kind of weather that isn't severe enough to stop people from packing up their umbrellas and towels and walking down to the shore.

I punch in the digits I know best on the phone.

The backyard is dominated by this oak tree. One summer, when Rose and I were little, Dad had taken the week off from work to build us a tree house. It was very childlike, with a crooked sign that read "Club House." It also had a thick white rope with knots spaced out every inch or so, used to climb up to the tree house's trap door. Rose and I thought it was the coolest thing ever. But as the years went by, and Rose went to college, and I was diagnosed with cancer, the tree house was abandoned, and was victimized by the rain and wind. Now its wood is all moldy and full of maggots, and the once white knotted rope morphed into a dirty brown vine. I don't go near it anymore.

By the second ring, Rose's sleepy voice answers. You know how it is with pregnant ladies. They cherish the gift of maternity leave by sleeping in until the late afternoon.

The conversation goes something like this:

Rose: "Hello?"

Me: "Hi, Fatty."

Rose: "Haha, very funny, Charlotte. I may be prego, but I can still kick your ass any day."

Me: "I would tell you to F off, but because you're pregnant and your hormones are out of whack, I'll give you the benefit of the doubt."

Rose: "Well, thanks Char. Considering that you just woke me up from my beauty sleep."

Me: "It's only 8:40."

Rose: "Yeah, but when you're on maternity leave, 8:40 a.m. becomes the new 5:20 a.m."

Me: "Wow, sounds like it's awesome to be pregnant and fat. Or both."

Rose: "Don't push it. What do you want?"

I suck in a breath, and deliver the news.

Rose: "A tumor?"

Me: "Two of them."

Rose: "But I thought you were in remission."

Me: "I thought so too. But the brain scan had a different story to tell."

Rose: "So that's it? The doctors can't do anything to save your hearing?"

Me: "I wasn't really left with a choice, Rose. If I don't go in for the surgery, there will be a 'fatal outcome,' as my doctor told me."

Rose: "And when you do go in, you'll come out deaf."

Me: "Hearing or life. Give up one for the other."

Rose: "How did Mom and Dad handle the news?"

Me: "Not too well, actually."

Silence.

Rose: "Aw, shit Charlotte. I don't know what to say."

Me: "It's okay if you can't pick out the words yet."

I change the subject.

Me: "How's the Addict?"

Rose: "Don't call him that."

Me: "Why? He's addicted to that Crackberry of his every time I see him."

Rose: "Yeah, well, he's out of the house buying milk and such."

Me: "Milk and such. *Very* descriptive."

The thought made me smile a little.

Rose: "Hey, is Dad's tree house still there?"

Me: "Yeah."

Rose: "Wow. I remember you and I would always fight for ownership of that thing."

Me: "I know."

Rose: "I have some good memories in that tree house."

Me: "Me too. But it's starting to fall apart."

Rose: "Maybe it's time to tear it down."

Me: "Yeah. Maybe."

8

To convey the tone of a violin is not always simple. A violin has rules of its own when played.

Rule 1: A violin can sound human.

When the bow glides down the violin's strings, the tone almost sounds human. If you listen carefully to the song being played, you may discover the violin's sound is familiar. For example, you can hear arrogance by pressing down on the strings. By swiftly striking the strings and producing low cuts on every high note, you can make the violin's "voice" sound greedy and uptight.

Rule 2: The violin's expression depends on who is playing it.

If you are happy, you can express your happiness through the bow, which will transfer it to the violin, which, in turn, will harmonize your feelings. When you are sad, your violin's bow slowly travels across the strings and turns the emotion into a pitch. Every person translates his feelings in a different way, and so every violin has a different sound, a different emotion and a different character.

Rule 3: When a certain emotion wants to be expressed there is a certain way to translate that emotion to the violin.

If you are feeling dull, you make the violin sound weak in its frequency. If you are feeling harsh, you put pressure on the upper midrange. If you are feeling gentle, you play the bow and strings the same way. In doing so, every sound you make falls into place to create a story.

Rule 4: Listen to the violin.

Just as the violin has the ability to express human emotions, the sounds it makes reflect what a person might feel when listening to its music. Listening causes the feelings to sprout. They cause the listener's feelings to swirl. Mostly a musician thinks about a person's emotion, and through her instrument, translates those feelings into sound. Sound takes a form before their eyes.

You have to "feel" the music, but as I said first, you have to hear it.

To this very day, I still don't get it.

Andrew, my brother–in–law, has always been an asshole.

How is it that he and my perky, popular sister hit it off so well?

Their relationship isn't exactly a match made in heaven, but I try not to care when that asswipe is around my sister.

I thought surviving my first adolescent years with Rose was the equivalent of surviving a nuclear war. But having Andrew marry into this family was like, waking up to a zombie apocalypse.

When I was fifteen, Rose first brought Andrew home to meet the family.

He didn't come anywhere near me.

No hello. No handshake. No smile. No wink. No nothing.

I remember him just standing in the doorway awkwardly, with his arm wrapped around Rose's waist.

I didn't know if Rose had told Andrew about my condition, since that might have explained the reason he was distancing himself from me. Maybe he was just ignorant to the fact that YOU CAN'T CATCH CANCER. It's genetic, not airborne. Yet that was dumbest excuse I could come up with for an explanation. My next hypothesis was that he was probably shy. So, raised in a family where being polite was like a practiced religion, I thought the nicest thing to do was strike up a conversation with him.

While Mom and Rose were setting the table, and Dad and Andrew lounged in the living room, I approached him when Dad got up to get a drink.

"Hi," I said. "So, Rose tells me you're an economics major."

He looked at me, his expression unreadable.

Then he turned his eyes away from me and stood up to follow my dad into the kitchen.

What the hell? I remembered thinking.

Then when we took our seats at dinner, I felt more comfortable and confident speaking to Andrew again. Rose was in the middle of telling Mom one of her stories from college when I finally turned to Andrew and asked, "So, where are you from originally?"

He looked at me lifelessly. He didn't say anything for what seemed like a really long time, until he realized that the table had gotten quiet waiting for him to answer my question.

"Santa Barbara," he said.

"Oh, where in –"

"Hope Ranch," he answered abruptly without even glancing at me.

Asshole . . .

It wasn't like I asked him if he did drugs in high school, or if he was ever arrested by the cops. In high school, Rose brought home the weirdest boys ever. One of them I think was high on shrooms because when my parents' backs were turned, he pulled out a bag from the secret compartment in his jacket, and offered me a piece of a chopped mushrooms. I politely declined the offer, but at least the Shrooms Guy was more talkative and well-behaved than Andrew. What agonized me the most was the fact that my parents or even Rose didn't notice Andrew's rude behavior.

So you might have guessed how *glad* I was to hear that Rose and Andrew were getting married. And you can just imagine the *joy* I felt when we had to travel to Santa Barbara for Andrew's family gatherings.

So after the wedding and after I met his side of the family, and found that his nieces and nephews were just about as judgmental and impolite as Andrew was, I wrote up a plan of how to survive with Andrew in our family.

I avoided being around him and his family members at all costs. Once we had to drive up to Santa Barbra for an Easter get–together, hosted by Andrew's family. I had recently recovered from a surgery that removed three tumors from my arm. While sitting at the dinner table, I reached over to grab a biscuit and I heard someone shout: "CHARLOTTE!" Andrew, sitting across from me, stared at my scarred, and bruised arm. "JUST ASK SOMEONE TO PASS THE PLATE TO YOU!" His nieces, next to me, giggled into their napkins.

I didn't know how my parents could see Andrew differently than I did, but they were obviously in love with him and his family, which really made me sick.

The next challenge for me was to not take his remarks seriously. When Andrew officially first learned that I had cancer, he might have been a tad bit nicer to me. However, I failed to notice the difference between Andrew's criticism and his attempts to joke with me about my cancer. He might have been trying to lighten my mood, but as a fact, I actually lost more and more respect for him. During another family gathering, he commented on a cluster of scars on my wrist from a recent surgery. He had a few too many drinks and thought he was being funny.

"Are you depressed, Charlotte?" he asked me, jokingly, but I found this uncomfortable. "Are you like one of those goth kids who lock themselves in their rooms and slash at their wrists or something?" *Fuck you*, I wanted to shout at him. But I just sighed and said: "Yes, Andrew, I am a little bit depressed today. Maybe it's because you just reminded me that have cancer. Thanks. Now which way is your grandma's bathroom, so that I can finish cutting myself?" Thank God no one was around to hear, but that shut him up for the rest of the day.

I guess the best way to describe Andrew, other than being an asshole, is that he's very manic. One day he could be all smiles and the next day he would snap at you if you rested an elbow on the table. I guess in the world of Andrew, he grew up in a family that raised him to believe that perfect was the norm. If you weren't perfect in Andrew's eyes, then that just gave him an excuse to treat you like an outsider. So I was at a disadvantage. For Andrew, it wasn't *normal* to routinely check into a hospital almost twice a month. *Normal* for Andrew did not involve tumors. I did not fall under his definition of *normal*. Within Andrew's sheltered life, *normal* was cancer-free.

But what has been the greatest mystery to me is why Andrew and Rose are still together. When you think about it, the two are completely different people. Rose is outgoing and fun, while Andrew is rude and stubborn. It would be the same as a weight sinking a ship.

Maybe it's something that I can't see. Because evidently, Rose sees something good in Andrew, and Mom and Dad see Andrew as their son.

But judging Andrew by what I've seen gave me the right to state my own opinion about him:

Andrew is an asshole.

THURSDAY / FRIDAY

At least I'm not the only one who is suffering in the ICU.

Nurse Frizzy wheels me out of my room.

We pass Grandpa Death's door, where a family of four—a mother, father and two little girls around the age of six—gather around his still body.

Cancer Kid has a lap desk resting against his knees, and he's scribbling something down on a piece of paper.

Cast Chick is gone. She must have left yesterday.

I'm in an okay mood today.

I still can't hear, so you know, that pretty much sucks.

Dr. Days drops by to visit me.

She signs to me.

Her sign language is better than my mom's.

Two week recovery. You still good?

Sure, I sign. *Have I missed anything of importance since my ICU isolation?*

Not much. Some celebrity couple got divorced. The new Wii came out. Apple and Amazon stock went up. And a new vampire book hit the shelves today at bookstores.

Nurse Frizzy comes into my room one afternoon to inform me that a vase full of roses was supposed to be delivered to me, but unfortunately the ICU enforcers don't allow flowers into patients' rooms. They're probably afraid that the roses are contaminated with some mutated pollen or something. Either way, when I ask my nurse who they were from, she says that the flowers were from a Melanie Gaukler.

I make a mental note to thank Mel for the flowers.

The next day, my parents stop by to see me, only this time, Mom brings along her mirror and make-up bag.

She signs poorly, *Here to make pretty.*

I haven't seen my reflection in five days.

Mom hands me the mirror.

The face staring back at me looks delicate and puffy. My head is swathed in a giant white bandage. Underneath the layers, I know, is a round, shiny bald skull with two new scars behind both of my ears.

I remember bringing Lexi with me into the hair salon and explaining my condition to my hairstylist. Lexi had watched in utter horror and fascination, as the hairstylist sat me down in the swirly chair and cut away large chunks of my blond hair until I was left with a very short pixie haircut.

When I went in for the surgery the surgeons then shaved away the rest of my hair before operating.

Furthermore, I lost so much weight in those five days.

It is shocking, seeing my sad eyes looking back at me.

I say nothing as Mom proceeds to apply rouge and lip-gloss on my face.

Dad sits at the foot of my bed and watches Mom beautify me.

When it is time to leave, Mom leaves the mirror in my room.

The color returns to my cheeks, and the eye shadow makes my eyes look larger and brighter.

I lower the mirror.

The make-up on my face gives the illusion that I am all happy and cheerful.

Well, I'm not.

I am actually still pretty miserable, and Mom knew it when she saw me, though she believed that she could cover up my sadness with a touch of eyeliner and mascara.

I think of Lexi and wonder what she would say if she were to see me like this.

Lexi . . .

I hit the red call button.

Nurse Frizzy returns!

Yes? She signs with a smile.

Do you know if a girl by the name of Lexi Abbott has been trying to see me?

Nurse Frizzy signs to me that she'll be right back.

Five minutes later, she walks into my room.

The nurse at the front desk told me that a certain Lexi Abbott has been coming by every day in the afternoon.

When can I see her? I sign.

Not for a while, unfortunately, Nurse Frizzy frowns. *But by the way the nurse described her to me, she seems like a very determined young lady.*

She is, I sign.

I then remember someone else.

Has anyone else come by to ask about me?

Like who? Nurse Frizzy signs.

Like a boy?

Again, Nurse Frizzy departs and comes back a few minutes later.

No, she signs.

Okay, I sign back.

9

"Wow . . . that sucks," Lexi sighs when I break the news.

Lexi and I are slurping highly-caffeinated chocolate frappuccinos in Spreckles Park.

In the park's gazebo a troubadour is playing while kids and families ride their bikes and fly kites. The sky is blue and the sun is warm, but inside me, it feels like it's twenty degrees below. We've been sitting on a bench for what feels like hours. I gaze at every toothy child and loving parent. No amount of caffeine is going to help. The depression attaches to me . . . like a tumor.

I used to love coming to Spreckles Park when I was little. It is five blocks away from our house, so it is an easy walk. On the weekends, Dad would always take me out of the house to this very park while Mom cooked us dinner. He would chase me around the playground, and we had this great father and daughter moment where we would go to the swings and he would push me. I felt like I was free whenever I was on that swing. Dad would push me so hard that I believed I would be tossed into the blue of the sky and fly over cities and houses. And as the swing swung back to him, I would beg *I want to go higher! I want to go higher!*

Now, it's a place of total discomfort. Lexi and I sit in silence for a moment. We have shared our love of music since we first met in the third grade. Call us the dynamic duo of music. The Tom Sawyer and Huck Finn of melodies. The Rocky and Bullwinkle of instruments. It almost makes me wonder if Lexi is upset more for herself or for me. After all the years of walking from school to her dad's recording studio to compose duets with my violin and her piano, Lexi probably feels like she's being cheated, too, by life.

"So, what are you going to do?" she finally asks.

I shrug.

"My boss is counting on me to help her." I turn to Lexi. "She wants me to see these two bands and pick one of them for her MS benefit."

Silence again.

Lexi nods her head.

I lean forward on the bench, kicking the stones at my feet. "I'm not sure if I'm even going to do it."

"You're *what*?" Lexi glares at me. "Why the hell *wouldn't* you take this job? People would literally kill for what you've been assigned to do. Kill, do you hear me? With a capital 'K.'"

"I'm really not feeling –"

She doesn't let me finish setting up my pity party before she rips into me again.

"Quit bitching about it to me!" Lexi nearly shouts. "Wake up, Charlotte, and hear the music!"

She snaps her fingers in front of my nose. "Come on! Ever since I met you it's all about the music with you. In the recording studio: *Lexi, go an octave higher.* Or: *Lexi, softer on the keys next time.* You love this kind of stuff. Calling out on musical mistakes and pointing out the obvious. You never say, *I'm not sure.* That's not the Charlotte that I know. The Charlotte that I do know would say, *Fuck this shit. I'm Charlotte Goode, bitches.*"

Her eyes are dry and her tan skin isn't pale with sorrow anymore. I've never seen Lexi this determined before.

Maybe it's the caffeine talking. Then again, maybe it isn't. Maybe it's Lexi being Lexi, telling me as a friend to stop whining like a little bitch and get back on my feet.

"You're right," I hear myself say.

"I'm right?" Lexi raises an eyebrow.

"Sure you are. I have to stand up and win myself back! In the past two days all I've done is cry, cry, and cry, some more! I also went on a Klondike Bar binge, so that wasn't helpful."

I take another sip from my frap, letting the memories of the musical relationship between us beat inside of me.

"It would help, I mean, if you came with me to the auditions."

She turns to face me.

"One last musical adventure between us?" Lexi eyes me while poking at the un-crunched ice in her frap.

"I would like that. No —"

I stop myself before reconsidering my words.

"I would love that."

10

If a tree falls in a forest and no one is around, does it make a sound?

Does it matter if you know it's falling?

If you stick me in a forest and I am already deaf and then a tree comes falling, of course I wouldn't hear it, but I would see it falling.

At least I can draw on the experience of having once heard a tree fall.

So in a way, if a tree were to fall in a forest, for me, it would make a sound.

Dr. McCord has been the family doctor for as long as I've been alive. He is the doctor who introduced me to my cancerous life and recommended Dr. Days as my oncologist. To this day he's overly pessimistic and cuts through the bullshit by stating his own opinion first about a certain topic.

Mom scheduled an appointment with him, to get a second opinion about my life-changing surgery.

I hate Dr. McCord's office.

The walls are painted with different colored dinosaurs and his carpet is stained with the mysteries of what little children have left behind. A low table with a five-piece puzzle and dried out markers and broken crayons remains a mess. The bitten heads of Barbie dolls and a legless Lego character in the toy bin stare at me.

I feel a certain kinship with the headless Barbie.

"I must say, I disagree with Dr. Days' decision of postponing Charlotte's surgery," Dr. McCord says. "From what she showed me of Charlotte's MRI scans, the tumors seem to be abnormally large. I can only imagine how much bigger the tumors will get in the following month, let alone how the tumors will interfere in her day–to–day life."

Mom's hand rests on my leg. "Well, Charlotte, her father and I have talked about the school situation."

This is true. Yesterday, after coming home from Spreckles Park with Lexi, my parents sat me down to discuss their plans of pulling me out of school. They told me straight up that they have no idea of how long I would be out of school, but the decision had to be made. For a few minutes when my parents introduced me to this plan, I was against it. After all, I was hoping to complete my junior year of high school on a high note. However, my parents did bring up my health. I myself had no idea how long I was going to need to recover from the surgery, let alone calculate how much of an effect the tumors would have on my school life. Who knows, I might be walking down to my locker but then convulse into a seizure. I wouldn't want my classmates or Lexi to see me spaz out on the hallway floor. So, we decided unanimously that leaving school was the right move to make.

"I'm still not convinced that this is the proper way to be treating a situation as delicate as this," Dr. McCord states. "I guess my only advice to you, Charlotte, is not to stress yourself."

All I want to do now is to go home.

Play my violin for two hours.

Listen to a good portion of the songs on my iPod, and sleep.

But Mom has a surprise for me after we leave Dr. McCord's office.

"Mom, whose house is this?"

Our black Toyota is parked in front of a white house with red trim. It is a tiny house; the type of house where I would expect to find my grandma on the porch in a rocking chair knitting a sweater. If she weren't dead, that is.

Mom kills the engine as she opens the car door. I follow behind her.

"This is Dr. Days' house," Mom answers when she opens the white gate for me and we approach the porch.

"Dr. Days' home?"

"Dr. Days called me yesterday to say that she knows someone who can teach you sign language. So I scheduled a meeting with her."

"Sign language?"

Say goodbye to multitasking!

I immediately picture all the things I won't be able to do simultaneously. I'll have to put my fork down when eating to answer a question at the dinner table, drop my toothbrush in the sink, let go of the phone . . . well I guess I won't be *talking* on the phone because I wouldn't be able to hear anyone on the other end, but I would have to start becoming more of a texter than a caller.

I had thought my misery scale hit rock bottom right after meeting with Dr. McCord, but, instead, it plunged even lower.

Mom knocks on the door and in seconds, the door clicks open and there stands Dr. Days. I am surprised to see her wearing a dark blue sweatshirt that reads San Diego Chargers and grey sweatpants. She is wearing normal clothes! People clothes, instead of her white doctor's coat that she usually struts in! I fear that the apocalypse is upon us.

"Oh, Mrs. Goode, Charlotte. Hello. Please come in." Her serious doctor expression is entirely absent. She smiles as she closes the door behind us and invites us to sit in her living room.

"Make yourselves at home. I'll go get Kilda," Dr. Days gestures to the couch before turning back into the hallway.

The couch is strangely comfortable, comfortable in a way that almost scares me, like Gretel in the gingerbread house before the witch tries to shove her into the oven.

Dr. Days returns.

"Charlotte," Dr. Days is holding the hand of a skinny old woman. She has short black curly hair that is lopsided on her skull. It looks more like a wig.

"This is my aunt, Kilda Patterson."

Because of my polite genes (which I never asked to inherit), I hold out my had to the old woman, expecting her to shake it.

Instead, Aunt Kilda looks at my hand, then up at me. She raises her free hand and gives me a salute.

"Um . . ." I am unsure of what to do next. Why was this senile old lady giving me a soldier's welcome? Then Kilda lets go of Dr. Days' hand. She turns toward me, still smiling. She places one palm over the other and moves it across the other palm gently. She uses her two pointer fingers and draws them together before pointing directly at me.

"Uh . . ."

"It's okay, Charlotte," Dr. Days smiles. "Kilda is just signing to you."

Kilda steps forward. She smells like dust and roses.

"Hello," she finally speaks in a raspy voice. "Nice to meet you." She then shakes my outstretched hand. I notice that the skin on her hand is sagging a little. She greets me with a small grin.

"Uh . . . yeah. Same."

"Aunt Kilda here is going to help you learn sign language," announces Dr. Days. "I talked with your parents about it, and they thought it would help you immensely."

"Very much indeed," Mom smiles. "Don't you agree, Charlotte?" She nudges me hard in the side of my ribs.

"Ow . . . yeah great. That's wonderful."

Dr. Days walks over to the kitchen, and brings back two chairs, placing them in front of the couch.

"Ms. Patterson, where did you learn sign language?" Mom asks, suddenly intrigued with this old woman who is going to stuff my brain like a teddy bear at Build-a-Bear-Workshop. Only instead of fluff, I was going to be stuffed with hand shapes and signs.

"Oh, I first started to use sign language to communicate with the deaf, wounded veterans during the Vietnam War. It was a requirement at the time when I was a nurse."

Mom, Kilda and Dr. Days talk about Kilda's history with sign language, while I sink lower against the cushions in boredom.

I wonder if it's possible to sign "Fuck you."

11

I am the only one in the entire restaurant thinking of a better color for the walls than a dirty pink magenta. Seriously, the manager, who let me into this restaurant, must have been color-blind when he picked the colors for his wall. On my schedule it says that the two bands are to meet at four o'clock at Brigantine on Orange Avenue. Mel told the manager to leave the place empty but to expect some band members coming over to use their stage.

If they arrive.

It's now four thirty and I'm like ready to paint the walls a different color.

I finally see a familiar figure sprinting through the glass doors of the restaurant.

"I'm so sorry I'm late!" Lexi huffs. "Car had a flat tire. I had to run ten blocks from my house to here." She looks around the empty restaurant. "Where are the bands?"

"They're not here."

"Not here?"

"Yup."

"Well then, we won't hire them if they're not on time."

Right, I think. *Because why would I hire someone who is wasting my precious time? Oh right, because it will be the last thing that I will ever hear.*

"Who do they think we are? We're running a business here, aren't we? What are the names of these tardy bands anyway?"

"Well, one of them is named Lennox," I say. "And the other –"

The entrance's bell rings and Lexi and I look in the direction of the door. Lexi looks horrified as a cluster of boys parade their way inside the restaurant.

Four boys walk in together. No one else.

"You from *Musique*?" one of the boys asks.

"Yes, this is the right place," I answer halfheartedly. I am still pissed that they came in thirty minutes late, but holding that against them with the limited time that we have doesn't seem particularly productive. "So, what band are you guys from?"

"We're the Bond Boys," one of the guys announces.

"Um . . . maybe I should call the other band," Lexi suggests as she grabs the folder from my hand. "You know, just to know where they are."

But before I can answer her, Lexi dashes away to the bar.

I turn back to the four boys and launch my professional speech. As I explain the details of the audition, I can't help but feel my skin prickle every time I mention the word *music* to them. As in: "I am interested to hear what . . . *music* you guys will be playing." I'm not proud of this. They drill me with questions, many of which I don't want to answer if it is a question directed to either their instruments or the songs that they would perform. But I figured that if I didn't have my disease, I would be swept away in the excitement of this job rather than having the words: *Pay attention to what you're hearing. It might be your last* plays continuously in my head in a girl's sing-song dialect "I-told-you-so" melody.

Once the talk of music and instruments dwindles down, it is time to let the band members take out their instruments and begin their audition.

Though being a professional means to *be* a professional, I find myself outside the restaurant just in case the Bond Boys need help with their equipment. Mel would have been proud if she could see me now. Outside, on the street, three of the boys help one of the band members with his drum set, while the fourth band member struggles to pull his instrument from his trunk.

I run to his side.

"Hold on, hold on," I say as I bend down next to him to retrieve his guitar. It is trapped underneath his amp, and if he pulls it one more time, it is likely his guitar will split in two. In his trunk are CDs of the Sex Pistols, a pack of Tic-Tacs and three unopened packs of 5 Gum. On top of it all are four editions of old *Rolling Stone* magazines.

"Here, lift the amp up and I'll try to pull it out."

The band member nods and reaches over to lift the heavy amp over his guitar. Slowly, I take the guitar by the neck and pull it out smoothly from under the grip of the amp.

It is a nice guitar, jet black with a purple and blue checkerboard strap.

"Thanks," he replies as I hand him his guitar. "I should be more careful where I put my things."

Yeah, stupid. Your guitar would have snapped like a toothpick if you yanked it one more time and my head would have been served on top of Mel's desk and used as a pencil cup.

I look up at the guy. He is a square–jawed teenager with reddish-brown hair and apple green eyes. He has a nice enough smile, tiny dimples at the corner of his lips and he smells faintly of Abercrombie and Fitch cologne.

I smile stupidly until my eyes travel down to his guitar. "Hey, is this a Vox guitar?" I quickly point to the instrument.

He looks down to his guitar. "Yeah," he smiles to me.

"It's a Mark VI," I babble, "because of its teardrop shape."

Shut up, Charlotte, my thoughts hiss at me. "They're mostly found in Kent, England, and were used by Brian Jones of the Rolling Stones. But many people confuse them for a Mark XII."

"Wow," the guy laughs. "You sure do know your instruments."

"Yup." My nails dig themselves into the center of my palm. "My friend's dad owns a record company on Coronado. He has an entire wall dedicated to a bunch of different types of electric guitars."

"Oh, yeah. I think I've visited that place. Crown Records, right?"

"Yeah!"

"Well, I'm very familiar with Crown Records' legendary wall of guitars." He holds out his hand. "I'm Ron Cam, by the way."

I shake it, smiling up at him.

"So I guess we should go back inside." He swings the checker-board straps over his shoulder. "Maybe we can hang together sometime and talk some more about guitars. Who knows, maybe we will agree on the difference between a Phantom XII and a Tempest XII."

"Yeah, sounds fun," I say. "We should make a date of it."

I feel my face grow hot.

Wow, Charlotte. You've really got this professional thing down.

I watch as Ron taps his fingernails against the hip of his guitar. "Okay then," he nods. "We shall."

He walks past me and goes through the doors of the restaurant.

12

Back inside the restaurant, the first thing that comes to mind is: *Where the hell is Lexi?*

As if she's read my thoughts, she suddenly bursts out from nowhere and plops herself down next to me at the table facing the stage.

"Apparently, Lennox called Mel's office . . ."

"They didn't show up," I roll my eyes. "Guess we're not hiring them then."

"What?" Lexi squints her eyes at me. "Doesn't that sound a bit unfair?"

"But you said it yourself before the Bond Boys walked in," I remind her.

"No. I said we weren't going to hire them if they're not on *time.*"

I stare at Lexi, trying to figure out what's going on.

"Alright, well we should at least help the Bond Boys set up their drum set."

Lexi's eyes grow wide. "Music execs don't schlep second rate bands' equipment."

Before I can protest, Lexi has leapt out of her seat and disappeared into the restroom.

At six o'clock, the Bond Boys leave the restaurant after their three hour audition, and Lexi and I begin our walk home.

"Charlotte —" Lexi says. "Promise me that you won't pick this band."

"Excuse me?"

"Well, I mean, promise me that you won't pick the Bond Boys until you've heard the other band."

"But Lexi –"

"Just promise *me*, Charlotte."

Lexi coils a strand of her black hair around her finger, her habit since the third grade.

"Remember that time after school, when I told you that I didn't want to go to my Dad's recording studio because the band there was being jerky?"

"Yeah?"

"Well, the Bond Boys were that band."

My body pivots in front of Lexi. "Seriously?"

Lexi gives a shuddering sigh, "A while back Dad left me in charge of the studio and the Bond Boys came in. I was only gone a sec—just for a *sec*—and I return to the sound lab where I saw one of the band members stuffing his guitar case with cables."

"*Just* cables?"

Irritation flickers across Lexi's face. Her carefully waxed eyebrows rise and her eyes burn into my forehead. It is the same expression she uses whenever she states the obvious.

"Yes, Charlotte, *just* cables," Lexi nods. "Think again. Think, more like thousands of dollars worth of wires."

"Oh."

"Yeah."

"So they were basically stealing from you?" I press my hands together.

"No. They were *stealing* from me and my dad," she allows herself to preen briefly at the word "stealing." "Anyways, so I catch these bastards red handed and they make up this lame excuse that one of the members misplaced his old wires and wanted to borrow some of the studio's wires."

Lexi continues to walk. "I didn't want to hear these guys lying to my face, so I did the next logical thing I could think of."

"Which was?"

"Kicking them out."

I gape at her, "You, yourself, kicked them out?"

"Yep, I watched until I saw their little hunched up figures scurry to the sidewalk."

"Wow…"

"Yeah, but Dad got all pissy at me when he returned to find the studio empty. I told him what happened and he just yapped on and on, saying that I had no authority to throw his clients out on the street, blah, blah, blah. So he made me apologize to them."

I don't know what to say, because I don't know what to think. I look at Lexi and her little angry body, but then I think back to Ron. He didn't seem to be the swiping type of guy. He just seemed to be some guy with a really messy trunk, a Vox guitar . . . and apple green eyes.

SATURDAY / SUNDAY

For the past two days, Cancer Kid's door has been closed.

I fear the worst, until one day Nurse Frizzy rolls me out of my room for lunch and I finally see Cancer Kid.

His door is open, and he has a black case resting on his lap.

At first I think it's a tiny coffin for a doll but then I recognize the shape of the case.

It's a violin case.

"Stop," I say, but can't hear.

Nurse Frizzy pauses in the middle of the hallway, and I sign to her that I want to visit Cancer Kid.

She rolls me into his room.

Nurse Frizzy says something to the kid.

The kid raises his eyes to me.

She signs, *This is James.*

He must be twelve or thirteen. He is connected to so many tubes: an IV in his wrist, a cannula in his nose, a heart-rate monitor pinched to his finger.

I can relate. I looked just about the same as him when I woke up from my own surgery. A fly caught in a web of pipelines.

His skin is a papery white, and his skull reminds me of a perfectly round poached egg.

When Nurse Frizzy authorizes the removal of the bandages around my head, we will probably be twins. In fact, I want to strip off the layers from my head to show Cancer Kid that we are in the same boat.

I want to tell him, "Yeah, this sucks spending an entire lifetime visiting the ICU because the cancer won't go the hell away."

However, I don't know how to say that in sign language.

So we gaze at each other, in silence.

On his bed are the sheets of paper that I saw him writing on his lap desk a few days ago.

Except these are not words and the paper isn't even college-ruled. It's sheet music with hand-drawn notes in between the lines.

Cancer Kid writes music?

I indicate the sheet music. *May I see these?*

Nurse Frizzy translates my message to Cancer Kid.

Cancer Kid nods.

I pick up the sheet music and read the notes on both the treble clef staff and the bass clef staff.

After many years of playing duets with Lexi on my violin, we always composed complex rhythms and note durations, like we were Mozart and Beethoven themselves. And even though most of our music came out sounding like crap, we thought we had just written the next great *1812 Overture*.

Cancer Kid's notes are simple.

The lower-pitch notes on the left to the higher notes on the right are written in ascending order.

I tear my eyes away from the paper, and in a matter of seconds, I realize that I've returned to the silence.

Cancer Kid is still looking at me.

He moves his lips.

He wants to know if you play an instrument, Nurse Frizzy translates.

"Violin," I say.

He does too.

A sudden wind of depression hits me.

Where is my violin?

Mom probably had it stored away since my surgery, with the expectation that I might not ever play it again.

I can't say that I blame her.

There's a chance she might be right.

Yet, I still miss holding that wooden body up to my chin.

He wants to know if you would like to play something for him.

I began firing off countless violin pieces that I've played in the past:

Bach's *Violin Concerto in A Minor.*

Bartók's *Violin Concerto No. 1.*

Vivaldi's *D Minor.*

John William's *The Imperial March* from *Star Wars.*

And many, many more . . .

But I end up shaking my head and lowering my eyes.

I feel Nurse Frizzy pulling me out of Cancer Kid's room.

I still keep my eyes down when we make it inside the elevator.

I'm thinking of the notes that I read on Cancer Kid's sheet.

Then I realize something as soon as the elevator doors slide open.

For the first time since my surgery, I had heard the notes that were written on Cancer Kid's sheet.

I didn't even hear any music.

13

Today, the world has gone mad.

First, I come downstairs and see my pregnant sister and her husband in the entranceway. Suitcases and bags are littered around them as Mom and Dad help them slip off their coats. As soon as my eyes meet Rose's, her face lights up and she hobbles over her Louis Vuitton suitcases to me. As she squeezes her arms around my waist I think her plump baby bump is going to give me the Heimlich.

"Charlotte," Rose flashes her pearly whites, "I've missed you so much!"

I watch her fold her fingers on top of her perfectly round belly.

Talk about having your own armrest . . .
I look over her shoulder to catch Andrew's eyes, but he is paying more attention to his Crackberry than to me.

I should mention, Andrew and Rose already have a child: BlackBerry, programmed in 2011 and now turning three years old.

"Hi Andrew," I say sweetly, for my sister's benefit.

"Hey," is all Andrew says, still glued to his gadget.

"So what are you doing here, Rose?"

My question is supposed to convey interest, but even to me the tone sounds whiny and unwelcoming.

"We invited Rose and Andrew to stay with us before your surgery," Dad answers, taking Rose's bags.

Before my surgery?

"So Rose and Andrew are staying here for the next twenty-six days?"

"Yes, Charlotte. And for God's sake, sound more appreciative that your sister is back in town," Mom says in an irksome tone.

I suddenly feel hot, like I am suffocating under several layers of wool sheets.

Next thing I know, I'm taking my jacket off the coat hanger and running out the door.

I hate pity.

Pity is a lie.

Usually when someone pities you, they say "I'm sorry." They give you flowers or cookies while you're still in the hospital, or "get well soon" balloons or a portable DVD player while you sit up in your bed pathetically looking at some ugly hospital wall art. You think that it's all nice and sweet of them, but under the surface, you know they're selfish. They're selfish because what they're really thinking is, "I hope I don't end up like *her*." I know the drill.

The Anderson family across the street once sent me markers and paper, and my classmates and teachers delivered tiny pots of plant–grams. And I was all like, "Thanks guys for showing your obvious pity in front of my face. Go spread it when your grandma dies."

Lexi is the only one who doesn't fall into that pity trap. When she knows that I have something bad, she never apologizes or gives me any gifts. She tells me outright, "Wow, you're totally fucked," and then we go back to prank-calling the freshman class.

Clayton's Coffee Shop has a walk-up counter service. I sit alone sipping a mug of black French roast.

Reality sucks, I think to myself. *God sucks. Andrew sucks.*

If only I had a giant eraser that could undo all of my problems. Life would be so much easier.

Suddenly there's a tap on my shoulder.

I swivel in the chair and come face to face with a square-jawed teenager holding up a bouquet of yellow roses.

My mouth goes dry. "Ron?"

He lowers the bouquet and turns to me. Ron is taller than I remember, and his eyes appear to have grown greener.

But Lexi's voice from last night invades my thoughts, and I swivel quickly away from Ron.

"Don't like yellow?" I hear him chuckle.

"Trying to bribe the judge, I see," I respond swiftly.

"Maybe," Ron laughs. As I watch from the corner of my eye, he swirls himself into the empty seat next to me. "They were on sale."

He drops the yellow bouquet in front of me.

"Why are you here?" I raise my eyebrows slightly.

"The truth?" Ron smiles broadly, exposing a row of bleach-white teeth. "Those flowers were actually for my mother's birthday. But then I saw you through the window. You looked so . . . serious. So I thought maybe something bright and flowery would cheer you up."

"Yeah, but aren't you afraid what your mother might think of you when you return with no flowers? Especially on her birthday?"

"She'll understand. Besides, I bought her a backup present anyway."

I watch as he reaches into a plastic bag hanging from his wrist. He pulls out two Coronado calendars and slaps them on top of the bouquet.

I can't help but cringe as I look down at the bent plastic of the two calendars. They came from the drug store down the street. I know because last winter when Rose and Andrew were staying with us over the holidays, Andrew forgot to buy me a Christmas present and BS'd his efforts by buying me a Coronado calendar for only a dollar. He was in so much of a rush that he forgot to remove the price tag when he wrapped it.

"That's great," I lie. "Sure she'll love it."

"Yeah. Maybe I should get one for Lexi as a peace offering."

I face Ron and watch him comb back one of his curls. His dimples disappear into a frown.

"What do you mean?" I ask.

"Well, my band and I know Lexi from that recording studio on First Street. But for some odd reason she seems to dislike us. *Especially* me." He leans and takes the calendars out of my way.

"She doesn't like *you*?"

"Well, the story goes like this. Last week, I left my cables at home, so my band and I used some at the recording studio, but I guess Lexi thought I was stealing some of her dad's stuff and threw me and the guys out. I tried to tell her the situation. I also understood that she was just looking out for her old man."

He leans back against the chair. "You're her friend, right? It's like some people aren't good enough for her."

I pick up my coffee. "Come on, she's not *that* bad, is she?"

Ron is quiet as I finish my cup.

"Maybe you two have gotten off on the wrong foot," I suggest.

"You're probably right," Ron nods. "Maybe you can, I don't know, grease the wheels for me?"

"How so?"

I look up into his green eyes. The morning light plays against Ron's dimples and curly hair. "Tomorrow, I'm hoping you can meet me in front of Crown Records," his expression made his face glow. "My band and I have to record a few tracks. Lexi's going to be there, and it would be great to have a friend to buffer things. That's if you're not busy tomorrow?"

Hmm . . . tomorrow, I think. Rose, complaining about her backaches. Mom, fussing over my hair. Dad, constantly asking me if I'm okay. Andrew . . .

"No, I'm not busy. I'll meet you there."

Take that reality!

14

I have always thought of Crown Records as my own little musical sanctuary. Lexi's dad used to let Lexi and me into his soundproof room to test out all the musical trinkets he stored. The place was stunning.

According to Lexi, when her dad first established his record company, he had this idea of designing a really high standard interior inspired by French bourgeois houses. Everything in the waiting room was imported from France. Carved pieces such as ladder–back chairs, armoires and tables served as the foundation of the style of Louis XIV. You can tell because the elegant furniture has gentle curves, rectangular shapes and a color that is almost sun–kissed but not faded. So while you're standing in this pre–French Revolution waiting room, and you go through the doors to the recording studio, you come face to face with all the modern-day electronics.

As I had told Ron, Mr. Abbott had an entire wall dedicated to different types of electrical guitars from all over the world. It was like being inside of a museum. The only difference is that there was nothing separating you from the guitars on the wall. Unlike in a museum, where a plate of glass prevents you from getting too close to an object, Mr. Abbott actually encourages people to touch and experience the feel of the guitars on his wall. His belief is that by touching an instrument, a musician will immediately know if the instrument is right for him or not.

But I remember entering the soundproof room with Lexi, and closing the door behind us. It felt like there was only one world, one fragment of the universe still in orbit: music. There was always an unlimited supply of instruments that Lexi and I could play with. A piano, guitars a drum set . . . the world was ours, all in this one building that might as well have been our private little French kingdom. But that was before Dr. Days dropped the bomb on me.

"Char!"

I look ahead. Ron strides toward me, his copper curls bouncing above his eyebrows.

"Glad you could come. No trouble, I take it?"

I remember the scene as I left the house. The family gathered in the living room to play Scrabble. Rose noticed me and asked if I wanted to play. I said no, explaining to her that I had to meet someone before lunch. Besides, Rose beats everyone at Scrabble, which makes the game less exciting. I mean, how many people seriously know what the word *Faqir* means?

"Nah, no trouble at all," I say.

"Good, good," he claps his hands together. "Shall we go in?"

He gestures to the Crown Records door. As I walk past him, he lowers his arm over my shoulder.

I feel a blush creep across my face.

Ron opens the door and we walk in.

Frames of records and pictures of musicians who have recorded here decorate the sage green and cornflower blue French walls. The other members from Ron's band sit on the leather couches.

He re-introduces me to his band members, Cole Winebread and the twins, Nick and Ty Shrew, without taking his arm off of me.

The door to the lounge room opens and Lexi stands in the doorway.

"Bond Boys – " she grumbles, but then she looks directly at me.

"Charlotte?" The blush spreads across her cheeks. "What are you . . ."

Her eyes drift to Ron's arm which is still around my neck. She looks annoyed.

Her reaction makes me uncomfortable. I feel exposed, almost nude.

"You okay, Lexi?" Ron tilts his head, his tone very light as if he was comforting a child.

Lexi bites down on her lower lip.

"Matthew is almost done," Lexi speaks slowly, through her teeth. "It will be another five minutes if you boys have the patience to wait that long."

"It's obvious that someone didn't sleep at all last night," Cole jokes. The twins Nick and Ty snort with laughter. Ron glares at them and his band members quiet down.

Lexi locks her eyes on me, "Charlotte, can you help me with the monitors? Like, right now?"

I slip from under Ron's arm straight toward Lexi. She slams the door behind us.

In the sound lab there's a mixing console, monitor speakers and a MIDI workstation. A window overlooks the soundproof room.

"Fuck tarts," I hear Lexi hiss under her breath. Her normal voice returns as she marches over to the mixing console and flips on some switches.

"Running the studio all by yourself, I see," I chuckle casually.

Lexi doesn't look amused. "Dad is out on his lunch break. Says he'll be back in a couple of minutes."

Lexi pulls back her rope of braided hair and swings it over her shoulder. "If you don't mind me asking, what are you doing with *him*?"

"You mean Ron Cam?" I correct her as I check the multitrack recorder.

"Whatever. The point is, what are you doing with him?"

"He invited me over."

"He invited *you*?" Lexi narrows her eyes at me. "You're not dating him, are you?"

"I don't think so."

"Well good," she presses a big red button that echoes her voice to the musician in the soundproof room. "Okay, Matthew, ready to try again? This will be the last one of the day."

A voice over the speaker answers, "Okay."

Lexi turns to me, "Look, I'm just going to speak my mind about this situation. I've worked with Ron and his douche band for the past two months. They'll sweet-talk you into anything. The first time they met my dad, they just bought him over with shitty complements and such. Next thing I knew, he was signing them up to record at this studio." Her face turns a bright red. "Just use your brain, okay. Don't get all girly and flattery with him, like some stupid ho."

"Well, you don't have to worry about me," I reply sharply.

Why are you such a jerk? I think as I slip the Bose headphones over my ears. *Maybe Ron is right. I guess he and Lexi don't get along. She's never been this pissed before. And stupid ho? Where the hell did that come from?*

I'm searching for the volume when I look up and see Matthew, the musician, in the soundproof room. He's wearing a black leather jacket and sitting on a bench with his fingers on the piano in front of him. He's facing ahead, singing as his fingers fly across the ivory keys. The room fills with a sound so complex and yet so slow and beautiful that it catches me off guard. I feel unsettled, yet I feel like I can easily drift away and get lost into the air.

And then –

The musician looks up quickly. I spin around to find Ron standing beside me, bashing his knuckles against the glass.

"Hey!" Lexi throws the headphones off her ears.

"Look Lexi, I know Matty is your golden child and all, but come on. We paid for this hour!"

"Wait your goddamn turn!"

"ALEXANDRA!" We all turn to see Lexi's dad in the doorway.

"I believe these gentlemen have an appointment for eleven. Why then are they not recording when it's now five minutes past?"

Lexi scowls.

"Well go on, get them in there!" Her dad gestures to the sound-proof room before he marches into his office with a brown Taco Bell bag.

"Charlotte," Ron says, coming up to me and resting his hands on my shoulder.

Lexi turns away from me, her braid whipping against her neck.

"After we're done recording, would you mind if we all take you out to lunch? You've been so patient with us, listening to our god-awful music. It's the least we can do. You in the mood for Burger Lounge?"

His apple green eyes shimmer.

"Sure," I smile.

Lexi stands with her back to us and slams some dials on the mixing console.

The door opens and Matthew walks out of the soundproof room. He stumbles on the pile of wires before catching his balance. Ron and the rest of the Bond Boys circle past him.

Lexi pushes her bangs away from her eyes and takes a deep breath before turning to the musician.

"Charlotte," Lexi finally smiles. "This is Matthew Lovelace. He's from Lennox."

I whip my head around. "*Lennox*? You mean, from the other band?"

He is hardly handsome, with those furry eyebrows and gangly posture. His arms sway at his sides, almost twitching.

"So you're part of the band that didn't show up to our meeting?" I address him.

His smile falls and he looks down, "I had to take care of my sister all week. She was sick." His voice was deep and full of sympathy.

"Then where were your other band members?"

"Touring in La Jolla. But what they really do is just barhop from town to town."

"I see," I say. "Are we to expect you and your band anytime soon?"

"Yeah, we called your boss to reschedule our meeting with you tomorrow afternoon."

"She must have been pleased to hear about your tardiness."

"Not going to lie, she didn't sound too happy. Then again, I wouldn't be either if a band suddenly didn't show up."

"Me *either*," Lexi hisses, her eyes staring forward at the Bond Boys in the soundproof room.

"Alright then, I guess we'll see you soon," I say.

"My band and I will be prepared," Matthew nods, as he rushes out the door.

"You know, you were pretty good in there," I say to him as he leaves.

But he's out of earshot to hear me.

15

The notes hum on my fingertips, the air inked with the sensation of sound. It is just me and the violin in this room. With my bow, I paint all sorts of images. I can feel them in my fingers and see them in my head. My fingers ache as I clutch the neck of my violin, this time with more power as I swoon and tip my bow in different directions, my wrist growing heavy. The vibrations against my cheek linger in the air like perfume as I lightly slide the bow down on the last note.

"Will you shut that *thing* up?"

Surprised at Andrew's appearance, I jump before slamming the bow to my side.

It is seven in the morning, and I have gotten up early to play.

Andrew stands in the doorway of the living room in his red boxers and white nightshirt. His blond hair is in tangles and he glares at me.

"Sorry. Did I wake you up?"

"We're trying to sleep," he exhales slowly. "Can't you practice later today?"

I remind him that I am seventeen and just one year away from being legally emancipated. But in my mind I shout at him. I imagine hitting him over the head with my violin and screaming for his ill sensitivity.

Let me play, you douche! I imagine myself saying. *Don't you know that all the sounds I've loved and grown up with are ticking away? Can't you understand? Do you understand?*

God, I can't believe I am breathing the same air as Andrew.

I turn my back to him.

I walk up to the front door and swing it open.

The morning breeze greets me as I step outside and close the door behind me.

My destination is unknown.

"Charlotte?" Dr. Days' is astonished when she sees me. "And your violin . . ."

I look down in my hands and notice that I ran six blocks to Dr. Days' house with my violin and my bow clutched in my red fingers. Worse, I now only realize that I am in my robe and slippers.

What am I doing here? I had to get away from Andrew and I wind up on the porch of the next most annoying person that I can think of?

"Sarah, who is it?" Aunt Kilda croaks from inside.

"It's Charlotte!"

"Oh, she's early today! Bring her in quickly, Sarah!"

Sarah?

It never occurred to me until now that I never knew Dr. Days' name. To me, Dr. Days' name was just an unthinking title that my parents and I would say.

We're going to Dr. Days.

Dr. Days says to take these pills before you go to bed.

Drive carefully to Dr. Days' office.

It was as mindless as saying trick-or-treat every time someone answered the door on Halloween.

I walk into the house and Dr. Days sits me down on the couch. She strides into the kitchen, filling a teapot with water.

Aunt Kilda walks into the living room, her short, black wig sideways on top of her scalp. Her eyes drop down to my instrument straddled across my lap.

"I take it you play the violin?" she says, staring.

I frown, "Yeah. But I'll have to stop when I'm deaf."

Aunt Kilda is silent, and Dr. Days watches this drama from the kitchen.

Aunt Kilda moves her the chair in front of me and slowly sits down. The veins on her hands remind me of spider webs.

"May I hear?"

I shoot my gaze at her, and in return, Aunt Kilda gazes back earnestly.

"You want me to play?"

The thought is tempting. I'm such a show-off, maybe one quick piece wouldn't hurt. I stand up and swing my violin to my chin and I adjust the strings before resting my bow above the first string. I play softly, closing my eyes, feeling the notes from my bow. I dip my bow to one side to start the melody again.

When I'm finished, I open my eyes.

Aunt Kilda's face is the same as before.

But Dr. Days is no longer in the kitchen doorway.

16

"Don't tell me you're joining one of the bands?" Lexi leans back in her chair, looking at the violin in my hand.

We are at Brigantine, waiting for Lennox.

"No, I spent the morning with my sign language teacher," I explain. "How long have you been here?"

"Not too long," she reaches into to her bag and pulls out a book. "I had time to visit Bay Books. While my car was getting repaired."

She hands me a glossy covered book. *The Art of Sign Language.* On the cover were the handshapes to the alphabet.

"I thought of you when I saw it."

Great. Now everyone will be thinking of me when they hear the words "deaf" and "sign language," and I'll have no idea what is going on.
"Is everything okay?" Lexi notices the twinge on my face.

"No, not really."

I put the book down and explain to Lexi about my sister being back in town, as well as her obnoxious husband.

"Is this the same guy who tried to joke with you about your cancer?"

"Yeah, pretty much."

"What an ass," Lexi says. "If he really gets to you, my doors are always open. You are more than welcome to practice at my house any-time you want."

"Thanks, Lexi." But I am still sick of the idea of sharing a roof with Andrew.

I change the subject. "How do you know Matthew?"

"Oh, he started early this month," she says. "He's super nice. A bit awkward at first, but interesting to talk to. He plays like three differ-ent instruments. Piano, guitar . . . or maybe it was just two. Anyways, I couldn't believe it when he told me that he was the lead singer for Lennox."

I don't say anything. I remember listening to the music he com-posed from the piano in the soundproof room.

Lexi then grumbles, "So how was your *date* with Ron?" She asks in the same deflated voice that she uses to describe what her mom has packed her for lunch.

Her eyes narrow into slits, and I consider not answering her question. All four of the band members were nice enough to ask how long I've been a part of the music scene in Coronado. I didn't mention my tumor or my surgery, I thought it best to not bring up something dark in an enjoyable environment. Instead I told them about my preg-nant sister and my annoying brother-in-law staying at our house. Ron genuinely seemed interested in my sister's pregnancy, questioning me about the baby's gender and agreeing with the snarky remarks that I had for Andrew. It was finally nice to hear someone share my dislike for that Crackberry addict. In the end, the boys paid for my lunch and Ron wrote down his cell number on one of the napkins.

"It was okay."

Lexi blinks hard, she looks irritated. I wonder if it was the word "date" that got her pissed off or whether she was disgusted with the image of her best friend and her worst enemy sipping a milkshake together at Burger Lounge.

"I always believed that you had a thing for *smart* guys. But never in a hundred years would I guess that you would be into someone who is *disingenuous*," Lexi protests in a low voice, looking down at the table.

I open my mouth to make a smartass reply, but just then Matthew and two other boys enter the restaurant.

"Sorry we're late," Matthew walks up to Lexi and me.

"Oh please, there's no need," Lexi's eyes skim over the two other members of Lennox. "Anyone who can perform as well as you, Matthew, deserves a standing ovation, not an apology. Right, Char?"

I don't answer as I observe the two other Lennox band members. One is a tall slender boy wearing an Iron Maiden T-shirt, a Metallica jacket and black army boots. He looks like he could be Jesus, if Jesus had a thing with metal bands. Next to him is a stocky guy wearing a blue-collar- button down shirt and a Homestarrunner cap. It was a good attempt to bring the hipster scene back into the world.

"This here is Xander Sayyid and Jeremiah Hendrix," Matthew wraps his arms around the two boys. "They're my band."

All I see is a piano player, a metalhead who might just be Jesus in disguise and a guy who has an army messenger bag decorated with pins from numerous indie rock bands slung cross his shoulder. What kind of music could they possibly make?

"Are you joining our band?" the hipster, Jeremiah, nods to my violin.

"Sadly, no," I reply.

"What can you play?" This time it's Matthew, his brown eyes resting kindly on me.

"Anything," I say. "Mostly stuff from Andrea Bocelli."

"Really? So you can you play *Por Ti Vlore*?" Xander asks.

I am taken aback. First impressions have a knack of surprising you when you least expect it.

"Yes," I answer the metalhead. "Yes, I can."

As soon as Matthew and his band gather on stage I immediately feel this urge to approach him and request the song that I heard him play yesterday at the recording studio. The experience from yesterday felt like I was falling into nothingness. It was nice for once being gravity's responsibility of just floating in peace. But I see that he pulls out his guitar instead of his piano and a wave of disappointment sweeps across me. However, it didn't take too long for the disenchantment to vanish. The band begins to play and Lexi and I listen. It is different. It isn't as dreamlike as the song Matthew played on the piano, but it wasn't bad at all. Just different. New.

Jeremiah has a steady beat on the drums, while Xander strums on his base guitar. Their tune is a beautiful, sonic whirlwind. It sounds like they were shooting arrows instead of playing their instruments. The song is swoopy, mysterious and danceable, characteristics that Mel is looking for.

The band ends its song and bows before their microphones.

Lexi and I applaud.

When Matthew raises his head, his brown eyes meet mine. He smiles.

He has some talent, I note.

He removes his guitar from over his shoulders and jumps from the stage to Lexi and me.

"Good work," I say.

Matthew moves close. I glance up at him, but I'm still sitting down. I drop my eyes to his feet, I notice he's wearing Nike tennis shoes.

"You really think so?" Jeremiah asks from behind his drum set.

I nod. I peek up to see Matthew. He seems tense, like he's bracing for the worst.

Suddenly, the doors to the restaurant burst open and I see Ron and his band walking in.

Lexi hisses, "What are *they* doing here?"

"Charlotte!" Ron is walking straight toward me, "How have you been?"

Immediately, he rests his arms around my neck. He looks at my violin on the table.

"I see you're thinking about joining our band. We could use a fiddle player."

"It's a violin, Ron," Matthew corrects him with a "you should know this" smile.

Ron's eyes travel to Matthew and his jaw clenches into a tight smile.

"Hey, Matty," he snickers. "I see that you've met Charlotte here."

He claps my shoulder, "Isn't she the greatest?"

I look up at Ron, who's glaring at Matthew.

"You should have seen her yesterday at lunch with the boys and me," Ron looks like he might breathe fire on Matthew. "She has such a charm, more charm than any girl *I've* dated."

Lexi now taps her fingers angrily against the table's surface.

"Forgive me," Matthew looks down at his watch, "I need to go." He glides past me, jabbing Ron with his elbow. Xander and Jeremiah exchange confused looks as Matthew slings his guitar case over his shoulder, and bulldozes through the door. Once again, he is gone.

"He'll be fine," Ron sighs. "So, are we next?"

MONDAY / TUESDAY

Round two.

It's been exactly a week since I've woken up from my surgery, and the first thing that I'm craving is a milkshake.

Not one of those cheap-ass ice slushies that the hospital cafeteria *claims* is a milkshake.

I mean a top-notch frothy ice cream shake you can ask for in any drive-thru restaurant.

I've signed to my parents to bring me one of those Burger Lounge milkshakes in a to-go styrofoam cup, but from my mom's glazed expression, she probably thought that I was signing for her to bring me a toothbrush or something.

Either way, no milkshake has arrived for me.

But something else came.

You have a visitor, Nurse Frizzy signs to me in the afternoon.

Great, the parents, I think.

However, a girl with long braided black hair enters the room instead.

"Lexi!" I smile.

She's wearing a visitor's badge and carrying an abnormally large, red shopping bag from Nordstrom.

Her lips move to say hello, as she pulls out one of the chairs and sits next to me, careful not to touch any of the tubes that disappear under my sheets.

She bends down and draws something out from the bag.

A magnetic dry erase board, like the one I used to have in my locker to write down homework assignments, rests on Lexi's lap. She uncaps one of the pens and scribbles something on the dry erase surface, before passing the board and pen to me.

How are you feeling?

The pen has an attached eraser tip, so I erase the question and write out my own answer.

Like shit.

I hand the board back to her.

This exchange goes on for a while. I feel like I am in middle school all over again, passing notes to Lexi between our desks while our teacher's back was turned.

Well that's to be expected, Lexi writes. *It is brain surgery, after all. Nonetheless, I still worried about you.*

I know, I write. *I've been in solitary confinement for like a week. I can't remember the last time I went outside. I might go nuts if the hospital doesn't release me soon.*

Well, your parents were very nice for allowing me to visit you. They updated me about the whole ICU protocol, so I know my time is limited.

My nurse told me that you stopped by a couple of times.

Yeah, but they wouldn't allow me up. Makes sense when you're still recovering from a life-changing surgery.

We write some more to each other, passing the board back and forth, and discussing the latest gossip that I've missed since being away from school.

Finally Nurse Frizzy pops her head in my room and says something to Lexi.

Lexi hands me the board.

Your nurse informed me that I have only five minutes left.

Okay.

I brought something for you. I kind of had to smuggle it into the ICU.

She pulls out a giant black case from the bag.

Not just any case.

My violin case.

I hold my eyes wide, at the very sight of my violin.

Lexi writes on the board, *I asked your parents if I could bring it in for you. I'm not going to lie, they were hesitant at first. They thought that it wasn't a good idea, but you know what, they don't know you like I do.*

I only stare at her message.

Lexi erases her writing, and writes something new.

You can still play the violin, Charlotte. Being deaf doesn't mean that you're incapable of composing music. Look at Beethoven. He was as deaf as an earthworm, yet composed the most badass pieces ever!

I know she means well, but the very sight of my violin case reminds me of the first thought I had when I saw Cancer Kid's violin case in his room.

I thought it was a coffin, and in a way, now seeing my violin before me, packed up in its black case, it made sense for me to think that my violin is dead.

For me at least, music is dead, and the very thought of hearing a sound is dead.

I feel a warm hand rest on my wrist.

I turn to meet Lexi's eyes.

She hands me the board. *Don't give up. Please, Charlotte. Don't give up on what you love to do.*

But I can't bear to write anything back.

Finally, Lexi writes me a new message.

He's been asking about you.

I feel my face flush.

I snatch the pen, erase Lexi's previous message and show her.

Where is he?

Touring with the band, she writes. *They won't be back for another week at least.* Then adds, *He's been trying to call your cell since the party. Either it's not on you, or you're not hearing it. Then again, that's not going to be helpful since you can't hear over the phone anymore.*

I remember that I had left my phone at home the day before the surgery. Electronics are forbidden in the ICU, but Dr. Days allowed me to listen to my iPod one last time before the surgeons wheeled me away into the operating room.

He wants to know how you're feeling, if you're okay. Basically, he has a lot of questions to ask you. Mainly, why you bailed out on him and his band the night of the party.

I remember that night so vividly.

Loud music, beautiful lights . . .

But I left the party early without explaining why to him.

I'll call him for you, to let him know that you're okay. Look, I know that you've already explained to me why you bailed the night of the

party, but you left without him knowing what hap-
pened. I'll try to get you guys to see each other
as soon as they release you from the ICU.

Okay, Lexi. I write, thankful that I have her as a friend.

Nurse Frizzy returns, informing Lexi that her time is up.

Lexi stands to leave, erasing my message from the board and inscribing her final message:

I love you, Charlotte Goode.

I write underneath her message:

I love you too, Lexi Abbott.

17

Mel doesn't betray any emotion.

"And?"

"And what?"

Mel sucks in a gallon of air through her nose and rolls her eyes at the ceiling.

"I got a call today," Mel says, "from the Swedes."

"The Swedes?"

Mel smiles.

"Oh my God! *The* Swedes?!"

Before I even started working for her, Mel has been trying to get a Swedish dealer to sell her magazine in Norway, Finland and even Denmark. It had been a long, eight-year project.

"What did they say?"

"Well," Mel's voice suddenly slows, "the previous Swedish distributor died suddenly of a heart attack and now her daughter has taken over the business. And quite honestly, she's a bit easier to negotiate with." Mel then mumbles, "Unlike that bitch who used to be her mother —" She takes a deep breath. "Anyway, the daughter wants to come to Coronado to see for herself if the magazine is worth selling."

Though this is excellent news, Mel sounds upset.

"That's great," I look up into her black eyes.

"Charlotte," the edge in her voice is suddenly razor blade sharp. "She's coming the day of the benefit."

"Right."

"And she wants to read the magazine's new article."

"Great."

Mel sits back. She covers her hands over her eyes and shakes her head. "You're not getting it," Mel narrows her eyes. "I can't show her the magazine because it's on hold."

I bite my lip.

Mel's palms slap her desk. "I mean the articles are done, the reviews are finished," she shakes her head, "but we still need a band for the magazine's cover and our main article." Mel frowns, "Charlotte, we can't wait any longer."

My blood goes cold.

Wait. Does she want me to choose already? Between the Bond Boys and Lennox? I can't do that! Not yet at least.

"I need your input, Charlotte. And I need it now," Mel's cold eyes dart at me, like an arrow piercing my chest. "I believed that you were up to this task."

I glance up at her, sinking my nails into the cushioned arms of the chair.

Mel isn't the most patient boss in the world, nor is she the nicest when it comes to deadlines. But what can I say? Both bands are equally good.

"You know, maybe I should take this out of your hands."

"But —"

"No, no. You've done enough already. I'll see if Katie Wang is up for the job."

Her voice is sharp.

I am rooted to my seat; I can't move, my right arm aches. I worry that the tumors have spread from my brain. I imagine a tumor forming onto the muscle tissue of my arm. This has happened before, on the tissue to my appendix. It was actually an easy surgery, since the surgeons had to take my whole appendix out to dispose of the tumors.

I suddenly blurt out, "I can finish it."

Mel sighs.

"I'll give you an answer."

"When?"

"How's tomorrow?"

Mel's face softens, "Very well. I'll expect an answer by tomorrow."

I close my eyes and nod my head in understanding.

As I walk out of Mel's office, the pain in my arm fires again. In the elevator, I try not to think about it as I push the button down to the lobby.

18

I wake up, with my brain feeling achy, and I need air.

I've been up all night trying to make a decision about the two bands.

Nothing seems to inspire me to pick one of them.

I play my violin in the morning.

It does nothing.

I go to Spreckles Park.

I can't find any peace.

And I go to Dr. Days' house for my sign language lesson.

Even signing to Aunt Kilda about how difficult my yesterday was doesn't comfort me.

Tomorrow is today. Mel needs an answer today!

All of this thinking blocks out the other stuff that is happening to me so far.

I forget to say good morning to Rose.

I forget to kiss my mom and dad.

I even forget to stick on my fake smile for Andrew.

My stomach growls.

Damnit! I even forget about breakfast and lunch.

I remember that Mootime is selling their cow burgers (their name for an ice cream sandwich) for $5.00.

Yummy.

Maybe if I get some food in me I can organize my thoughts.

It is a thirty minute walk from my house to Orange Avenue, and on my left I come across the silvery building of Mootime, which resembles a '50s diner. A rundown statue of Elvis Presley in a singing pose and a cow stand on each side of the door.

Someone walks out of the ice cream parlor.

Someone with Nike sneakers and a black leather jacket.

"Matthew?"

The boy stops and looks at me, his hands closing around a waffle cone filled with vanilla ice cream.

"Oh," he sighs. "Hey, Charlotte."

He doesn't look too surprised to see me, nor does he look happy.

"Um . . . how are you?"

"Good."

"How's the band?"

"Fine."

He seems to be scolding me with his caterpillar-thick eyebrows. For a second, I think one of his eyebrows is inching away to spin a cocoon.

"How are *you*?" he addresses me in a dense voice.

I'm not good! I'm freaking out here! I don't know what to do and I'm suffering from a major migraine or something.

"Hanging in there," I say instead.

Matthew's expression softens just a crack.

"Just hanging in there?" He actually looks concerned. "What's up?"

I spit out what's on my mind, "My boss is pushing me to pick a band by the end of the day, and I woke up with this really annoying headache that isn't going away."

Matthew's face becomes stony and his voice drips with thickness once more.

"Pick a band?" Matthew's brown eyes whip toward me. "It seems to me that you've already picked your band."

He stares straight ahead down Orange Avenue and begins walking past me.

"What do you mean by that?" I shout after him.

"Nothing," Matthew punches his free hand into the pocket of his leather jacket. "It's just the way Ron was treating you at Brigantine. It seems to me you've made your choice."

The back of my skull tingles. It makes me wonder if the tumors are growing faster. "The sad part about this is that you're going to let one guy blind you from the rest of us who actually want this job."

"Are you saying that I'm unfair?"

"You're not unfair, Charlotte. You're just stupid."

His words are like a slap across the face. And why is my arm suddenly tingly?

I take a deep breath, calming my nerves.

"I am not stupid," I say slowly. "And you shouldn't be talking to me like this."

"Or what?" he exhales loudly, rolls his eyes and walks off.

Or what? Or what!

I am beyond insulted! Matthew called *me* stupid! He doesn't have the slightest clue what I'm going through in my life right now! How dare he! Seriously! How dare he say those words in front of my face.

I whip out my phone.

Five minutes later, it's done.

I've given Mel my choice.

19

Mom wants Rose to come to my sign language lesson to meet Dr. Days and Aunt Kilda.

Immediately, Rose and Dr. Days click as if they were lifelong friends. Aunt Kilda just sits in her chair, straightening her wig.

I don't exactly hate the lesson, but it is a bit awkward to use my hands in odd ways in front of Rose and my mom.

Rose and Mom seem to learn a little sign language as well, by watching Aunt Kilda teach.

Faster than before, I ask a bunch of questions with my hands and am able to understand Aunt Kilda's answers.

Mom and Rose try practicing with me.

This is my first conversation with my family in sign language.

"Andrew. Sweetheart, watch this."

Rose thinks that she has caught her husband's attention at dinner when she looks at me to ask me a question in sign language. But I guess he doesn't know that in order to understand sign language you have to move your eyes away from your CrackBerry and focus on the hand shapes.

"Oh wow, that's really amazing, sweetheart . . ." Andrew responds in a monotonous pitch, but unluckily no one even looks at Andrew to see that his mind is completely absorbed by his BlackBerry.

Back and forth, Rose and I speak to each other by signing. Dad and Mom observe, amused. Andrew plays Brick-Breaker.

"Charlotte, I'm so proud of you!" Rose says, reaching for my hand. "You're going to make a perfect godmother."

All at once the silverware from both of my parent's hands suddenly clangs to their plates. Afterward the table is silent.

"What?" I ask, my pulse racing.

Had I heard her correctly?

"You want me to be the godmother?"

Andrew yanks his head up from his Crackberry to stare at Rose, appalled. Apparently he didn't give Rose the "okay" to make this decision, but I don't care.

She is looking at me again, showing off her straight white teeth.

"I know it may seem a lot to ask for because of your condition, but I'm not asking you to be the baby's godmother out of pity. I want you to be the godmother because you are my sister, and forever will be my sister —"

"Rose . . ." Andrew coughs under his breath.

I watch Andrew, his eyes focusing to catch Rose's attention, but she ignores him.

"You are a wonderful young woman, Charlotte. You're smart and thoughtful and I could never think of anyone better for this job than you —"

"Rose . . ."

"So what do you say?"

"ROSE!" Andrew raises his voice to grab Rose's attention.

Aggravated at Andrew, she snaps her eyes directly at him.

This shuts him up.

She then turns back to me, her face is plastered with a hopeful smile.

I am speechless. Since the day I heard that Rose was pregnant I have wanted to be the guardian of her baby. But I don't know how to answer her.

"Oh my God, yes!" I squeal.

I stand up from my seat and run over to the other side of the table. I embrace my sister thankfully in a hug.

"Thank you, Rose! Thank you!" I whisper in her ear.

Andrew rises to his feet and places his Crackberry his pocket.

"Excuse me," Andrew says tersely as he walks away from the table into the hallway.

The first thing I do is dig out the Burger Lounge napkin Ron had used to write down his number for me when his band took me out to lunch. Since he was engrossed about the condition of my sister and her pregnancy, I thought it was right to update him first about my new status.

In my room, I get out my phone and dial his number.

It rings once before someone answers.

"What?" Ron's voice is unrecognizable.

"Um . . . hey Ron," I squeeze my fingers. "It's me, Charlotte."

"Oh . . ." He sounds irritated. "You need anything, Charlotte?"

"Guess what?"

"What?"

I could hardly keep the volcano of good news from erupting from within me.

"I'm a godmother!"

"Oh hey, that's great?" It sounds more like a question than enthusiasm.

"Is everything okay?"

"Yeah, yeah, I'm fine."

"I have great news for you too. Mel is probably . . ."

"Yeah. She already called."

"Isn't that great?"

"Yeah. Of course –"

"I picked you."

"That's great! Thanks, Charlotte, for everything." It sounds he is about to hang up on me.

"Wait!"

"Yes?"

"I . . . I was wondering, if maybe you want to hang out tomorrow?"

I am surprised by the uncertainty in my voice.

Why am I suddenly so insecure?

I wait as the other line goes silent.

What is taking Ron so long?

I begin to feel uneasy.

"Uh, I don't know Char, I've got a lot on my plate this week already," he answers, lowering his voice. "I'll call you when the time is right."

Before I know it, the line goes dead.

20

I am making my bed when a grenade explodes in my head.

Something smashes against the back of my skull as the air from my lungs vanishes from my chest. My right arm prickles in an endless chain of tiny bursts.

I scream to alarm my parents, but they're not coming fast enough. I sway to the staircase, just as my feet become heavy and I hold onto the railing to steady myself.

My throat begins to close until a sharp pain hits my stomach and I vomit on the first step. The smell is atrocious, so I vomit again, this time falling to my knees. The smell is suffocating me.

"Charlotte!" My parents sprint in front of me.

Who is that? Is that my mom?

I look up, but I can't see. My vision is suddenly blurry.

I hear something. A cross between a scream and a muffle.

I fall over, hitting my head against the wall.

I feel my muscles firing randomly into repeatable twitches.

I have no control over myself.

And in all honestly, I don't mind dying right now.

"Charlotte!"

Lights.

"CHARLOTTE!"

A scream.

Sirens.

My brain is on fire.

I scream.

But screaming makes the pain worse.

My vision is clouded by dark, warm colors.

I twitch in the grip of the fiery torture.

My hair.

My skull.

I am on fire.

I can't hear my own voice as I cry for help.

I thrash.

I suddenly feel numb.

The fire is put out.

I slip into darkness.

I lean over and vomit into the plastic bin at the side of my bed.

"Whoa!" I hear a voice. "Easy there now."

I cough my way to consciousness in the hospital room.

Lexi is next to my bed, holding the bin.

"Lexi?" I gag, wiping the loose chunks of vomit from my cheeks.

I see Lexi smile. "Bitch, you don't know how lucky you are."

She lowers the bin and wraps her arms around me. She doesn't stand too close, afraid that I might hurl on her.

"I thought you were a goner."

I raise my head. "What happened?"

"What happened? How can you forget what happened when you just had a fucking *seizure*, Charlotte."

Lexi's tone is so pedantic that I almost don't hear her say —

"SEIZURE?!"

I try to swallow but it doesn't work.

"How?" I catch my breath. "How did you get here?"

"I called the house to ask if you wanted to have lunch today, but your sister picked up the phone and told me what happened."

"But how are you *here*?" I try again, my throat feeling rotten and gross. "In ICU?"

"Nurses said that you were stable enough to have visitors. I came as soon as I could."

I glance at the IV stand on the other side of me. Relenting, I lean back against the bed and avoid Lexi's gaze.

"Where are my parents?"

"I think they're talking to your doctor," she says.

Dr. Days is there in her white doctor's coat and her red hair is pulled back into a ponytail.

Lexi had already left, leaving me to the mercy of my oncologist and my parents.

"It's getting serious," Dr. Days sighs, when my parents and I are alone in the room. "Lucky for you, Charlotte, it was a minor seizure."

Mom is holding one of my hands at the side of my bed.

"But still serious," my voice is hoarse. I'm not allowed to *drink any fluids* in case I *throw them all up.*

"Everything is serious now," Dr. Days frowns.

"Will I have the surgery sooner?"

I only have twenty days left. I brace myself.

Both my parents turn to Dr. Days, waiting for her answer.

"The decision is for your parents to make."

I didn't realize until now how much I'd been counting on living out the final days of my hearing.

"May I have a minute alone with my dad?"

Dr. Days nods and begins to walk out the room, but Mom is still next to me. "I need to talk to Dad."

Mom looks at me quizzically but then Dad nods to her, and she stands up and follows Dr. Days out the door. I wait till the door closes completely.

"Pretend that I'm not your daughter."

Bear with me, Dad.

"As a lawyer, I want you to negotiate with me," I clear my throat. "I'm given a month to keep my hearing before I go deaf. But then I have a seizure," I look up at him. "But I don't want the surgery just yet."

He slides his glasses back up on his nose, a common lawyer habit when he needs to stall to think.

"If you were my client," I hear the reluctance in his voice. "I would . . . try to get an order from the judge to prevent anyone, like your . . . like your parents, from forcing you to have the surgery before you are ready."

He bites down on his lip and stands up. He grabs the bars on my bed and leans his face down to mine. "However, you're not my client, Charlotte." He says it with so much pain in his voice. "I am your father. And I'll do everything in my power to protect you, keep you healthy, and I will fight to the death with anyone who interferes with that."

There isn't a trace of anger in his voice. There is only love.

I take a deep breath and make my voice light and relaxed.

"I understand and appreciate that you love me so much," my voice sounds faint but my words are clear. "But it's my life. I'm almost an adult and I am responsible for what happens next in my life. I would rather die than not have a chance to complete what I've already started."

The muscles on Dad's skin release their intensive grip.

"If I have one more seizure," I say. "I'll undergo the surgery immediately. No questions asked."

WEDNESDAY / THURSDAY

When I was thirteen, my parents bought me this really cool iPod docking station for my birthday.

It was designed to replicate an old-school glossy black boom-box. Beefy, it weighed about thirteen pounds and delivered excellent sound. Even upstairs when I synced my iPod, and blasted songs from Coldplay or The Smiths while I did my homework, I would be able to hear the words perfectly clearly whenever I would rush downstairs to grab a Coke before returning to my room.

I hauled that stereo with me throughout the house.

If I was helping Mom bake a batch of cookies for one of her board meetings, I had that stereo on top of the counter playing The Rolling Stones. Even when I went to take a shower, I would leave the docking station on the sink's marble surface and scrub my hair while the guitar solo from *Don't Stop Believing* echoed throughout the house.

I had that docking station with me for four years. Its paint began to chip after the number of times I'd bumped its giant body against the doorways in the house. And the left speaker got a slight dent in the center when I accidentally shoved the docking station off my nightstand during a restless night.

But one day my parents were out of the house for an annual fund meeting at my school. My iPod selected a David Bowie song and I pressed my finger on the volume button so hard that the peg underneath the button snapped off. Suddenly, my docking station shut down, and I spent the entire night trying the glue on the volume button.

Well, the peg kept snapping off, so I finally gave up and watched my docking station silently collect dust in the corner of my shelf for the next year.

My own peg was broken.

As I continue to sit in silence, I wonder if there is a chance Dr. Days could glue back the peg to my own volume.

More and more, I miss the days of hearing. And the icy realization that my violin case will end up just the same as my docking station — collecting dust, silently forever — made me wish that I could hear something just one more time.

My parents want me to write a letter to Rose.

Today they had sent me one of her many messages written in her unreadable cursive handwriting.

Dear Charlotte,

Blah, blah, blah . . . wishing you all the best . . . something, something . . . how are you . . . did she write "feeling" or "breathing?" I could never distinguish between her f's and b's whenever she added little loops and curls to her words. It is as if everything she writes in that horrid handwriting of hers is supposed to be a masterpiece, like she's freaking Shakespeare or something.

Andrew and I are doing great . . . okay . . . baby is doing good too . . . should be due in the next month or so . . .

I find it surprising that Andrew doesn't have the heart to write me his own letter. Rose is old-fashioned and believes in the tradition of envelopes and stamps; Andrew, on the other hand, is more technological. The least he could do is send me an email from that Crackberry of his. But I guess he has other better things to do.

Like, baby stuff.

Or at least it better be baby stuff.

I'm not going to lie, though. I miss Rose completely.

Even though it was hell at the house during her stay, she nevertheless was always beside me.

I wish she was with me now.

The next morning, with a lap desk and stationery littered around my bed, I write Rose a reply with what little facts I could decode from her scribbled questions.

Rose, I write. *Hi.*

I tell her about the surgery, how it was painless yet terrifying. There isn't really much that I remember from the surgery, other than listening to the last line of the song from my iPod before the anesthesia took over.

I ask her how big she is getting, and if the baby is forcing her to indulge in the delights of Jell–o or sticks of butter. At least that's what my Dad told me my mom wanted when she was pregnant with Rose. Sometimes he would catch her late at night sitting at the kitchen table, ripping the silver cover off a Jell–o cup and spooning up chunks of the glassy goo. Or, on rare occasions, he would find her unwrapping a newly bought stick of butter and taking a bite out of the buttery bar.

Pregnant people can be so weird . . .

I write away, and I spot a slight shift of movement by my open door.

I raise my head and, lo and behold, it's Cancer Kid.

Jim, John, Jamie? I don't exactly remember his name.

He peeks his head through the doorway.

His bald head reflects the florescent lights, and next to him is an IV stand on wheels, hooked into his arm.

He waves at me.

I wave at him.

I stow away my letter and grab the whiteboard and pen Lexi left for me from her visit.

Can I help you? I write.

Cancer Kid's tiny eyes scale my room, and he looks back at me.

Where is this kid's nurse? I wonder. *What's he doing here?*

He opens his chapped lips and carefully mouths the words: *May I come in?*

I wonder if any of the nurses have told anyone about my deafness. Cancer Kid must know, since anything that I asked was through sign language at our last encounter.

He shuffles in, slippers on, his green hospital gown brushing against his ivory knees. The IV stand trails behind him, like an unwanted shadow.

Finally his eyes fall to the foot of my bed.

He sees my violin case.

He points to it.

Yours? He mouths.

I nod.

He drags the IV stand over to the case and touches it.

"What are you doing?" I find myself suddenly ignited with annoyance.

Cancer Kid is surprised at my voice.

Just looking, his mouth tells me.

I uncap my pen and write in very large, bold letters:

WHY ARE YOU TOUCHING MY VIOLIN???

He cringes at my words, as if this too is a form of cancer.

He stares me, doe–eyed and lost.

I was just . . . I can't read the last couple of words on his lips.

I hold out the whiteboard and pen, and he inches toward the items. His fingers graze mine, and I feel just how cold his hands are.

He writes his message, shaking uncontrollably, before handing me back the board.

I was just wondering if you would play something.

I stare at his words.

A surge of anger takes me over.

Was this kid mocking me, or serious?

Either way, my fingers make it to the call button, and in a matter of seconds, Nurse Frizzy appears in my room and gives a quizzical look as to why Cancer Kid is in my room.

Come, come, I read the words off Nurse Frizzy's lips.

The boy reaches out a skeletal hand for Nurse Frizzy's uniform while his other hand loosely closes around the metal pole of the IV stand.

I watch as they both slip out of my room at a snail's pace.

I sit and stare down at the note Cancer Kid had written to me.

I was just wondering if you would play something.

I release a long sigh.

How can I? I ask myself.

And then I erase the board.

21

For three days I stayed at Coronado Sharps Hospital after my seizure and almost went crazy from staring at the Gladius ceiling panels and watching reruns of the *Duck Tales* cartoon. Three days in the hospital without a call from Ron. I don't even know if he's called me or not. If he did, what would he think of me not returning his calls? Or worse, if he saw me and my swollen eyes and hollow cheeks. Only three days, and I lost a pound a day. When I fell on the stairs during my seizure, I had smashed my cell phone.

This is the perfect excuse to make a quick trip to the store where Rose is buying me a new phone. Though both my parents and Rose encourage me to sleep more each day, I am always awaken when I think about the MS benefit and what little time I have left to listen to the things close to me. The minute I leave the store with my new phone, I check my messages.

I have one. From Mel.

"*I don't know why you're not picking up your phone and for some odd reason I don't exactly care.*" She sighs with boredom as if her

Starbucks drink is more important than me. *"But you have to come to the office tomorrow at five o'clock sharp. I need to discuss with you our plans for the upcoming draft of the magazine. If you do get this message, Charlotte, at least show up so that I can confirm you're still alive and breathing. That will be all . . ."*

Well, she sounds peppy.

After negotiating with my lawyer of a Dad, we agreed on a number of prerequisites if I was to postpone the surgery: first off, I can't drive anymore, which is certainly sad because I love driving and experiencing that whole sense of independence when it's just you and the car. Second, I have to wear an ugly seizure bracelet that jingles when I walk. If anyone asks, I'll just say it's some sort of charm bracelet. Yeah, that's likely to be believable. And third, I can't sit next to an emergency exit doorway on a plane. This is a shame, since the emergency exit row is the only row in the entire plane (besides first class) where you have the privilege to stretch out both of your legs. Nevertheless, I don't plan on traveling for a while.

But today, Rose is willing to give me a ride to work.

I get off the elevator with the black folder tucked under my arm.

I walk in and stride up to Mel's office. When I look through the glass windows of her office, I see her . . . smiling?

Wow, I think. *That seizure must have caused me to start hallucinating.*

Mel's head is thrown back, and her red lips expose her white teeth. There's a client sitting across from her. I've never heard Mel laugh before, but it sounds like a combination between a grunt and a giggle.

Her eyes flash in my direction as she waves me inside, still laughing.

I walk in and the "client" turns his head.

It's Ron.

Usually his shirts have a few unbuttoned buttons, and he allows his copper hair to be wild and messy. But not today. Ron has made a special effort to dress up. He's wearing a tucked-in shirt and blazer. In addition, his copper curls are pushed back over his forehead. And, wait . . . is that cologne that I smell?

"Charlotte!" Mel says. "How are you today?"

Good God! Did someone finally perform an exorcism on her? Or am I going crazy?

"Um . . . good," I answer quietly. "Ron."

"Charlotte," Ron replies. His tone is cold.

His apple green eyes move from my gaze to the walls to Mel's desk, and finally to an imaginary speck on his blazer.

"Hi," I can barely whisper.

He doesn't hear me.

"Well then, let's begin," Mel says.

I take a seat.

Mel goes into great detail about the upcoming issue of the magazine. 'Course, Ron's band will be on the cover, so Mel talks directly to him about photo shoots, interviews and record deals.

As for me, I'm writing down whatever Mel is saying in my black folder.

Ron runs his fingers along the leather of the armchair, listening and nodding.

I peek at him through the curtain of my hair.

Ron responds to Mel in a very businesslike fashion. He cracks a small joke between sentences and Mel howls with her grunt giggling laughter.

"Well, that's it," Mel prompts, standing up and concluding the meeting. "Oh, and Charlotte . . ."

Ron slips his gaze to his baby blue Vans.

"Good work by you."

Ron and I leave.

He is walking ahead of me. He didn't say one word to me after our minimal greeting.

Did I do something? I think. *Is he mad I didn't call?*

We're walking in the same direction to the elevator, so I decide to make some small talk as we wait before the sliding doors.

"So, how've you been?" I force a perky smile. But Ron just rubs the back of his neck.

"Um, okay," he sounds hesitant.

"So, I wanted to apologize for not calling you in the past three days."

"Uh . . ."

I'm officially on autopilot mode, and neglect to screen the words slipping from my mouth.

"I was actually going to call to ask if you were free on Friday."

The elevator bings.

The doors slide open and Ron dashes in with me behind him.

It is silent in the elevator for a few seconds. Ron coughs. "I'll check my schedule," he says. "Right now I'm not too sure. As you just heard, my band and I will be pretty busy with Mel for the next couple of days."

"Well, do you have any recordings coming up? I'm sure that if I have time, I can drop by and visit you and your band at Crown Records."

The elevator doors open.

"I don't know, Charlotte," he fast walks out the door and into the parking lot. "Now may not be a good time."

I watch him draw out his car keys. It takes me less than a second to grasp what he is saying. Although he had suddenly acted superior to me after Mel's meeting, I can't help but cling to him. I really don't want to lose him, and I vomit out, "CAN I HAVE A RIDE?"

I cringe as I say it. I sound so desperate, but I swear it sounded better in my head.

Ron turns to me. "You don't have a car?"

I scratch the back of my head, still sore from lying on my back for the past three days. I am actually supposed to call Rose to tell her to pick me up, but with Ron here, plans seem to automatically change.

"Um . . . no," I mumble.

Ron exhales, "You sure? You don't have a phone on you or something?"

"No," I lie, feeling the weight of the new phone in my pocket grow heavy. "I forgot it."

Assaulting my stomach is a mob of butterflies, and I regret ever opening my mouth in the first place.

Ron just stares at me. Contempt is written across his face.

He knows what to do.

The Jeep is flooded with silence.

Ron doesn't turn on the radio or roll down the windows. It's as if he is afraid that any sudden movement will cause the car to crumble.

He slows down when we reach my house.

"Thank you," I unbuckle my seatbelt.

"Okay," he mumbles looking straight ahead.

"See you soon?"

"Yeah." I sense the tint of irritation in his voice.

I open the car door and jump to the sidewalk.

The second that I close his door, the orange Jeep drives away.

What just happened? I ask myself while walking up the steps. *He's suddenly . . . different.*

I hear the glorious sound of arguments coming from the house.

I open the door, to find Andrew hovering over Rose, who's sitting at the dining table.

When they see me in the doorframe, they freeze.

A second later, Rose sighs and avoids my gaze, pretending everything was normal before I walked in.

"Is everything okay?"

Rose doesn't answer. She glues her eyes to the table's checkerboard placemat. Andrew looks at Rose for some information, but she doesn't raise her head to look up at either of us.

The response I get is silence.

That's when I realize that Rose and Andrew's argument had something to do with me.

And neither one of them is going to talk.

"Fine then," I hiss.

And I run back outside.

22

It is too quick of a walk from my house to the park. Within minutes I'm sitting on my usual bench across from the gazebo.

In the distance, the last layers of the afternoon sky bleed into the approaching dark evening clouds. It looks beautiful, but I'm distracted, reflecting on the events of the last four days.

I know that I should be concentrating on the beauty around me. The grass is greener, the clouds look like a painting in a museum. Yet my attention is circling in a continual loop. Ron never cared about me at all. Rose and Andrew. The seizure. My loving parents. Lexi and all of the musical sounds in the world. None of them can save me.

What can I do? Will I be able to face another day of pain? What if I can't? I hug my legs to my chest and squeeze them close, lowering my head on them. I am surprised that the tears do not come sooner.

I'm sick, my mind screams. *I'm sick! How am I going to survive?*

I can hear my sobs and even taste the saltiness of the tears running down my lips.

A wind picks up and the leaves from the trees rustle.

Another sound catches my attention. A low guitar pitch.

"Charlotte?"

The leaves hush.

I look down and see a pair of Nike tennis shoes.

"Hey, Matthew," I grumble.

The wind softens.

"Um…" he sighs. His guitar is slung over his shoulder. He's obviously been practicing.

There is no hiding it. "Sit down." It might as well be me who breaks the awkwardness. I have nothing better to do. I hope to God that he didn't see my crying.

When he sits down next to me, he slides his case underneath the bench.

"So . . ." Matthew trails, waiting for me to fill in the blank.

"So what?" I lower my legs and use my sleeves to wipe the remaining tears. Maybe he'll think that I have something in my eye.

"Well, you're crying . . ."

Damnit! So he knows.

I quickly change the subject, "Yeah, and what exactly are you doing here?"

Matthew looks down at his guitar. "I was practicing. Usually I need some fresh air, and Spreckles Park is very quiet in the evenings."

Indeed he is right. Not even the crickets chirp at this hour.

Finally Matthew looks back at me. "Look. I may not be your friend," he taps his guitar's body, which echoes a hollow sound. "But since we're here, do you want to tell me what's going on?"

The gulf of silence expands between us.

"I've been told that I'm a good listener," he hints with a soft smile.

Just like that, my voice gives way. "I feel like an idiot! I asked Ron to give me a ride after we went to my boss's office. I already had a ride, but I really wanted Ron to give me a ride. He hasn't called in forever, but then we were in the car and he just ignored me and I was trying not to confront him about it because I don't want to be too mean about it, but he seemed so tense when he drove me home. He looked really angry and I felt angry, but I didn't know what to do. I wanted to tell him that I had a seizure a few days ago but—"

"Oh my God!" he pulls the guitar strap over his head and rests the instrument on the side of the park bench. "You had a seizure? Are you okay? When did this happen?"

"Not too long ago," I avoid his gaze and talk to his tennis shoes. "I fell down the stairs when it happened. I hardly remember the details."

"You had a seizure!"

"Yeah . . ."

"So why . . . why the hell is Ron on top of your list of problems? You had a seizure! A seizure! And all you care about is some guy who probably can't point to Canada on a map!" Matthew's face goes from white to red as he rants.

I find myself smiling and looking up into his eyes. They are understanding, though he doesn't say he's sorry for me out loud.

I lose track of my words. Everything flows out of me so easily. I'm suddenly a bleeding wound.

I talk about the tumors.

My deafness.

My deadline.

The magazine.

"So that's how you met us," Matthew pieces. "Ms. Gaukler gave you the job so that you could feel like you've accomplished something with your hearing."

"Yup."

Matthew then tilts his head at me. "How many days do you have left?"

"Seventeen."

My good friend, the silence, returns. Matthew turns back to his guitar and picks it up.

"You want to hear something?"

I don't answer, but I watch as Matthew swings the strap over his shoulder and rests the guitar on his lap.

He gently glides through the strings, tuning the instrument, then clears his throat, "I've changed it a little. But it doesn't sound as good as the original."

He strums on one string, his tennis shoe tapping to the rhythm. It is a familiar beat.

Matthew begins to play that beautiful song that I first heard him record at Crown Records with Lexi.

As he plays, I look up at the sky. It is darker than before. The clouds are replaced with the faint stars overhead. In the background, Matthew's music makes a new world around me. The strings he plucks make the stars shine brighter, the wind cry louder and the air turn sweeter.

Matthew creates a new universe with his music.

He plays the last note.

Silence.

"I'm sorry that I said you were stupid," Matthew says.

I finally look back at him. My face doesn't betray my emotions.

"Thanks."

He glances down at his watch, "I should be getting home."

He jumps to his feet and draws the guitar case from underneath the bench. As I watch him rest his guitar in the case, I don't move. It's dark, it's cold and I don't want to be alone just yet.

"Will you walk with me?"

Matthew freezes for a second, then nods.

I stand up and together we walk into the darkness.

"My sister is cooking tomorrow," he says, swinging the guitar case to his side. "She usually makes too much for my parents and me to eat. It would be nice to have someone come over and help us."

"Wait," I stop and arch my eyebrows at him. "Are you asking me out?"

"No," Matthew smiles slyly. "I'm asking you to help my family and me finish my sister's cooking. There's a big difference."

But I can see the enjoyment beaming from his face.

It has been a very strange kind of day.

"Sure," I say grinning. "Not a crumb will be left from your sister's cooking once I'm done. I'll even lick the plate until it's spotless."

23

As Rose drives, I recognize everything we pass.

Coronado is such a tiny island, I've probably explored every street and beach while living here, with the exception of the Naval Air Station on the north side of the island. So there was a possibility that I had unintentionally driven past Matthew's house millions of times without realizing it.

Rose drives straight across Orange Avenue and continues on Seventh Street. The road turns sharply, revealing a new row of houses. Whenever I blink, it appears that each house is growing bigger and bigger.

"It's somewhere around here," I say to Rose. She slows down as I look back and forth from the address Matthew wrote on my palm—the previous night when he walked me home—to the houses on each side of me.

"Right here," I point to the house that matches the address on my hand, and Rose pulls up.

"See you at nine," Rose calls before she drives away.

My eyes stop on the house. This can't be Matthew's house. It is so . . . cute? Happy? I don't know. But just by looking at this house, a list of synonyms scroll through my head, each relating to "*comfortable*."

For one thing, it is a *big* house. Ginormous, more like it. Rectangular. Symmetric. And green.

I walk through the small gate, up the red brick pathway to the porch, and ring the bell. I don't expect the sound of the doorbell to be so loud.

The door opens and sure enough, there is Matthew.

"Charlotte!" he smiles. "Uh . . . hi. You're here . . . early."

He isn't wearing any shoes.

"I know. Hope you don't mind," I answer.

"Um . . . no . . ." he smoothes down his hair nervously. "No. But please come in."

He opens the door for me.

The hallway is very bright and large.

"This is an amazing house," I blurt. I just had to say it out loud.

"Thank you," Matthew replies and closes the door behind me.

Waiting to greet me, in the doorway to the kitchen, are Matthew's parents.

"Guys, this is Charlotte," Matthew's voice breaks the short silence as he introduces me.

"How do you do, Charlotte?" His mom steps forward, and greets me with a large smile as she hugs me. She's wearing large circular glasses and has perfectly high cheekbones. She shares the same brown hair and eyes as Matthew, and has a beautiful pixie hair-cut that evenly frames her face. "I'm Teresa Lovelace. Welcome to our home."

Behind her, a man who is the exact height as Matthew, strides toward me. He has handsome hazel eyes, a little white scruff around his cheeks and chin, as well as fluffy cotton candy gray hair. "Hello!" He shakes my hand. He has a nice, confident grip, "I'm Charles Lovelace. It's very nice to finally meet you. Matthew has told us much about you."

"Good things, I hope," I actually seriously hope that Matthew hasn't said anything bad about me during my drastic decision to choose the Bond Boys over his band.

"Oh, very good things, Charlotte," Mrs. Lovelace's wonderful large smile confirms that there is nothing to fear. But now it makes me wonder what exactly Matthew had told his family about me that made me out to be this "good person." I wonder if he told them about my disease?

"Where's Norah?" Matthew asks.

"I'm here!"

Matthew's parents split to the sides of the kitchen doorway. But instead of seeing a pair of feet, I see wheels.

Here is Matthew's sister, Norah, sitting in a wheelchair, leaning over the stove and stirring a steaming pot. It smells like pasta.

She turns her head and grips the top of her wheels to spin in my direction. She comes to a graceful stop in the doorway. She continues to hold the spoon, a string of pasta dangling from the end.

From the corner of my eye, I see Matthew's body stiffen as I gaze down at his sister.

"Hi Charlotte," she says enthusiastically, sticking out a hand, "I'm Norah."

I look down at her wheelchair, then at her heart-shaped face. She has caramel curly hair and twinkling amber eyes like Matthew's.

I shake her hand, "Pleased to meet you."

Unlike her father's, Norah's grip is faintly weak, yet she manages to give me a slight squeeze. "I hope you like Italian food," she says.

At dinner, Norah Lovelace says that she has MS.

I didn't ask her. She just chattered on about her weak muscles, her muscle spasms and the difficulty of moving her legs. It is as if she is reciting her day at school.

"I also have *nystagmus*," she turns to me, her elbow on the table. "Do you know what that is?"

"No," I smile at her. "What is that?"

"Okay," she lowers her fork and does these hand motions like she's reenacting a dramatic piece of gossip. "It's this really creepy thing in which you have involuntary eye movements. It's like a twitching in the eyes. Like this—"

And I watch her left eye vibrate uncontrollably in her socket.

I laugh, "Whoa, that's pretty cool."

Matthew coughs into his napkin.

"It's also why I have the wheelchair," she tells me. "You know how MS affects people."

She even shows me her bumper sticker on the back of her chair that reads:

LOST YOUR CAT? TRY LOOKING UNDER MY TIRES.

"I like cooking, too," she chatters, talking a mile a minute. "Even though I'm fourteen, Mom says that I cook like a pro."

And she is right. Norah has made all the food herself. She cut the tomatoes and grounded them into a sauce, stirred the pasta, buttered the bread and chopped the lettuce. I guess that I've failed Matthew, because ten minutes into the dinner, I am already stuffed and there are still three plates displaying the golden pools of melted butter from the pasta left on the table.

"We'll take care of the dishes, sweetheart," Mr. Lovelace stands up to take Norah's plate. "How about you go outside and get some exercise?"

Norah crumples up her napkin and drops it on her dish before wheeling herself away from the table.

"Nice to meet you, Char," she smiles at me. She looks at her brother. "If you want someone to finally finish eating all of my dishes, you seriously need to invite people more often, Matty."

She laughs while wheeling herself out of the dining room.

"Norah seems very enthusiastic," I say to Matthew. Teresa, Charles, Matthew and I are in the kitchen, washing and drying the dishes. "I like her a lot."

"Yeah. She has this way of making people like her," he says through tight lips. "It's like a gift or something. It's probably because she doesn't hide the fact that she has multiple sclerosis."

I go back to scrubbing the sauce off a bowl. When I look through the kitchen's window, I see Norah in the driveway. She is shooting a basketball toward the lowered basket by the garage. She jumps a little in her seat when she releases the ball from her fingers, and the ball flies then down into the netted throat of the basket. When the ball bounces to the ground, it rolls down the driveway past Norah. She spins in her chair trying to catch it. Just then a trio of girls walk past the driveway. One is tall and blond, the other two are short and brunette. The ball taps against the blond girl's ankle. She looks down at the ball and then back to Norah.

I realize my fingers are gripping the sides of the sink.

The blond girl bends down to pick the ball up. She turns to Norah.

Norah calls, "Evening, Chastity! How's your day going?"

The girl, Chastity, smiles, "It's too short for it to end. How about you?"

The girls and Norah have a long discussion, bouncing the ball to one another as they speak.

Finally, one of the girls ends the conversation and Chastity bounces the ball back to Norah. She catches it in her chair and waves good-bye.

"Charlotte," Matthew's voice catches me off guard, and I spin to face him. His brown eyes are on the bowl in my hands. It is overflowing with warm water and soap from the sink.

"Maybe I should wash for a while," he says.

24

So I am sitting at our regular booth at Burger Lounge. The one that looks on to Orange Avenue and across from Petco and the Pizza and Greek Grill. I want nothing more than to cross the street and hear the cars honking, or even stick my head into the pet store, just to hear the parrots' annoying squawks. Yet, Lexi called me this morning begging me to have lunch with her, and in all honesty, it is only fair. I mean after all, last time I saw her I puked into a bucket when she visited me in the ICU. Plus, she probably wants to know how I'm doing since my seizure.

This might be why I suggested meeting Lexi here. Burger Lounge is one of the few places where we can pretend that my life is normal and not ruled by my stupid disease. But now the surgery is only eleven days away and time is moving too fast. I almost wish for that magical stopwatch in that *Twilight Zone* episode where time literally freezes.

I could really go for that right now . . .

Last night, I had a nightmare that while I was sleeping, a team of nurses broke into my room and kidnapped me. I was laid flat on a kitchen table, not an operation table with the sheets and the anesthesia, but a table in which I could feel the crumbs from previous meals press into my back. And next to me was a smaller table with a pizza cutter and an ice cream scooper on it. A man reached for the pizza cutter and loomed over me. I tried thrashing my way off the table, but the nurses pinned my arms down to my sides. Before the blade touched my skull, I woke. Though it was only a dream, the reality was still to come.

Minus the pizza cutter, of course.

"Hey, Char."

I nearly jump at the greeting.

"Lexi!" a smile breaks across my face when I see my friend. "Well, just don't stand there. Park yourself right here and order something fancy. I'm paying."

"Yeah. A double-double with cheese is probably the fanciest thing in this place."

Lexi slides into the seat across from me. There is silence for a moment while she skims the menu. I glance past Lexi and look out the window.

"Six days," Lexi laughs.

"What?"

"Six days since I've last seen you. And as I recall, you regurgitated into a bucket."

"Yeah," I say. "I was hoping you wouldn't say that."

Lexi laughs, folding the menu away. "So, what have you been up to over the past week? Have you picked a band yet?"

Suddenly, I find that my lips are sealed closed. I can't look at Lexi or out the window without feeling that uncomfortable shard of guilt.

"You didn't hear?"

"Hear what?"

"Well, did Matthew or the Bond Boys say anything to you at the recording studio?"

"Oh, that," Lexi rolls her eyes and sighs before continuing. "Dad banished me from his studio after that last stunt I pulled on the Bond Boys the day you came in. Do you know what he said to me?"

I'm not paying attention while she curses about her dad or the Bond Boys or even the studio. I think she says "like" like 16 times in one sentence and I think she gets off track and babbles on about how she hates carrots or tomatoes.

"I'm sorry," I interrupt her as she's in the middle of complaining to me about why the sky is blue or something. "So, you haven't been at the studio in three weeks?"

"Nope," she pops her *p*.

"And you haven't heard from Matthew or the Bond Boys either?"

"*Nada*," she answers in Spanish. "What's this got to do with the auditions?"

I mumble an "Oh God," under my breath and close my eyes.

And very slowly I say: "I picked the Bond Boys."

"You *WHAT*?!"

The impact, I imagine, is the same as the hydrogen bomb going off. Because with my eyes still closed, I can picture buildings crumbling, windows shattering, people disintegrating and mushroom clouds forming.

"GODDAMNIT, CHARLOTTE!" Lexi explodes, slamming her fist against the table. "WHAT DID I SAY TO YOU?!"

I swallow and open my eyes. I feel like speech is impossible, but for Lexi's sake, she needs to know the whole story.

I force the words from my dry throat, "I was stupid, Lexi."

"The hell you were!"

"But I'm trying to make things right."

Lexi's scarlet face seems to pulse with anger every time she blinks at me.

She. Is. *Pissed*.

"What do you mean?"

I sigh, "I met up with Matthew after I picked the Bond Boys and we're sort of friends now."

"*Friends*?" Lexi's eyes charge at me, as if searching for some sign that this is a joke. "After you picked the *other* band?"

"Well, yeah. I was shocked too," I say. "And afterward I hung out with him more, and as time went by it struck me that I fucked up big time for this guy."

Lexi blinks. "What about the Bond Boys? Lost interest?"

"Actually I think *they* lost interest in *me*."

"And *Ron*?"

"You were right about him. He was just playing me."

Lexi shakes her head and sighs, "I told you so."

"You did. Over and over and over and over and over again."

"Who's the crazy bitch now?" Lexi finally puts on a gloating smile.

"Yeah, yeah, yeah," I wave away at her smile.

"So, whatcha gonna do?"

"I don't know." In truth, that is my best answer.

"You don't know?" Lexi repeats. The silence invades the room, and Lexi finally releases a low sigh, "Well, until you find an answer, Char," she says, not meeting my eyes, "I wish you the best of luck."

FRIDAY

Two days.

Just two days left!

You must be excited, Nurse Frizzy signs to me as she wheels me into the hospital cafeteria.

How could I not be excited?

I get to finally leave this dungeon of a hospital and be free!

As I sit down and slowly scoop up tiny spoonfuls of the hospital's mushy mashed potatoes, Nurse Frizzy takes a seat across from me and watches me eat.

She taps the back of my hand, and I raise my eyes at her.

What did James want with you? She signed.

James? I struggle remembering the face.

The boy who is sick, Nurse Frizzy signs. *He walked into your room yesterday?*

That's his name? James?

I put down my spoon.

He found my violin in my room. I sign. *He wanted me to play him a song.*

Why didn't you play him something?

I raise my eyebrows at her.

Shouldn't it be obvious?

I can't hear a damn thing.

When I don't sign back, the expression on Nurse Frizzy's face changes.

She finally understands why I couldn't entertain Cancer Kid.

I'm sure you can still play something.

I sink back into my wheelchair. Now I know what Norah feels like, always being cooped up in a chair on wheels, barely using your legs to maneuver between Point A and Point B.

Everything becomes limited when you're in a wheelchair.

Just like how everything becomes limited to you when you lose your hearing.

Mom and Dad stop by one more time to visit me.

I'm ready to get the hell out of this place.

Today Nurse Frizzy encourages me to walk around the hospital wing to reconnect myself with the feeling in my legs.

I almost don't recognize the floor beneath my feet. I sway and wobble a bit at first, and then I slowly begin to place one foot in front of the other and make it to the other side of the hallway in a matter of minutes.

I now know what the Little Mermaid felt like when she exchanged her tail for a pair of human legs.

Go around the wing one more time, Charlotte, Nurse Frizzy encourages me.

My strides are small, and when my knees buckle, I reach for the wall to keep myself from falling.

I pass Cancer Kid's door.

It's open and I see him sitting on his bed with his lap desk and sheet music littered over his blanket.

I stop and look at him.

He raises his head from his paper, and looks back at me.

We stare at each other.

Me, free from all the wires and IV drips.

Him, still plugged in with tubes.

I raise my hand and slowly wave at him.

He breaks off his gaze and returns to his sheet music.

He does not wave back at me.

25

For the next three days I am at Matthew's house.

Because of the deal that I made with Dad about abandoning all hope of returning to school, I've been spending more time at Matthew's house than at mine.

In the span of those three days, it feels like the current of time has compressed everything into a single moment. There is music, sign language and Matthew, though sometimes not in that order. Sometimes they merge into one big event in which Matthew asks me to come over to show Norah some of the signs I've learned while he practices the piano in the background. Matthew keeps asking why (with my newfound freedom) I always end up at his house instead of running off to the beach or taking the bus to Carlsbad for a day.

Usually, Teresa and Charles are out of the house when I come over to visit, but there is a plate of cookies wrapped in plastic with a pink sticky note reading:

For M & C. From T & C

I always visit when he come back from school in La Jolla. He prefers being schooled off the island, as to not get caught in a tiny environment like Coronado. Sometimes Norah is there. Her presence in the household is most apparent from the smell of her cooking coming from the kitchen. Every time Matthew welcomes me in, I smell the vegetables simmering with rosemary, spices or tomatoes. When Norah isn't cooking, she joins Matthew and me, telling us interesting facts about American history.

Washington hated being president.

A solider from the Union Army during the Civil War found General Lee's battle plans in the tobacco box of a fallen Confederate soldier.

Barrack Obama's thirteenth cousin is Dick Cheney.

When Norah isn't present in the Lovelace kitchen, Matthew explains that Teresa took her to a physical therapy class. Norah attended the same school as Matthew in La Jolla.

I don't see the importance of keeping track of the passing days. I suspend myself in the present. At Matthew's, my fingers clutch at the fabric of the sofa as if time is threatening to sweep me away. I refuse to look behind me, for it is too painful, and I avoid all thoughts of the future for fear of where I would be later on.

But as I wake up this morning, I encounter a very strange thing. My eyes open to the morning light melting through my window. There are no mourning doves cooing in the trees or the seagulls crying in the sky.

How strange, I think, *the world suddenly seems quieter.*

I lie in bed for an hour, staring at the ceiling. I watch as the morning shadows creep from my bookshelves across my floor. That feeling of doom isn't haunting me anymore. I look around my room, waiting for my emotions to pick up. I am waiting for that sense of realization that I am another day closer to losing my hearing, but nothing happens. In fact, I feel like the world is at peace. No one yells, cries or makes any noises. No one laughs, yawns or even snores. The world is suddenly a quiet one. I turn my head to gaze out my window to see what the weather is like. It's a clear fall morning. If it had been raining, would I have known without even looking? The branches on the trees sway in the wind. I don't hear the leaves rustling as I watch. My eyes provide me with the information that I need.

So this is what silence is like, I think blissfully.

"You can't keep coming here," Matthew says to me when he opens the door and finds me there standing on his porch on the fourth day.

"Says who?" I ask.

"Me," Matthew crosses his arms. "Do you really want to spend your last days of hearing listening to my crappy music?"

"Shouldn't that be my choice?"

"Yes, but I'm not going to lie, it's a pretty lame choice," he smiles at me.

"Well then, what do you think I should be listening to instead?"

Matthew rolls his eyes up to the doorway and sighs.

"How much money do you have on you?" he asks.

"Twenty dollars," I say. "Why?"

"Perfect. Go around the house and meet me in front of my car." he says.

Matthew slams the door, and circles back to the garage where his white Subaru is waiting in the driveway.

He finally locks the back door, but slung across his shoulder is his guitar.

"Hold this," he hands me his instrument as he fishes for his keys and motions me into the car.

Matthew drives while I ride shotgun with the wooden guitar across my lap.

We speed over to Guadalcanal Road, where Matthew directs the car into the McDonald's parking lot, and finally pulls up behind a big red Honda in the drive–thru line.

"What are we doing here?" I ask.

"Oh, you know, getting a little afternoon meal."

"I don't eat McDonald's."

"Neither do I."

"So why the hell are we here?" I am getting annoyed, since the guitar is cutting off all of my circulation to my legs.

"So you can hear something amazing," Matthew answers, as the red Honda pulls up to the next window.

Matthew rolls the car next to the drive–thru confirmation screen, where an order board displays pictures of Chicken McNuggets and Egg McMuffins.

Matthew parks the car and adjusts his seat so that there is room between him and the wheel. "Hand me my guitar."

I pass the heavy instrument over to him.

As Matthew tunes the strings on his guitar, a women's chipper voice from the confirmation screen says, "Good afternoon, welcome to McDonald's, how may I take your order?"

"What's your name?" Matthew asks the screen.

"Um . . . Nancy," the woman on the other end sounds uncertain.

Instantly, Matthew begins strumming and singing.

"Nancy," he sings to the screen. "Can I get a Quarter Pounder? With extra, extra, extra, large fries, please?"

I can't stop myself, I start laughing. I cover my mouth just when the women over the speakers asks another question. "And what would you like to drink?"

Nancy sounds amused. And why shouldn't she be? How many people actually go to a drive–thru window with a guitar, to sing sonnets about McDonald's Quarter Pounder?

Matthew continues strumming and turns back to the screen, "I would really love to have a cup of your Premium Roast Coffee."

"What size would you like it in?"

"Large. Oh, I would very much love my coffee to be, be, be large."

This is so entertaining that I can't help but smile and wonder what Nancy must think of us.

"Alright, is there anything else that I can get for you?"

Matthew strums louder on his strings, "Two Chicken McBites!"

"Medium or large?"

"Medium if you would!"

"And do you want fries with that?"

"Fries, please, oh please, oh please!"
"And what would you like to drink?"

"A McCafé Mocha."

There is a pause, and then Nancy's voice returns. "I'm sorry, can you repeat that?"

Matthew stops strumming and looks directly at the speakers. *"A McCafé Mocha, please."*

His fingers continue strumming, and Nancy asks with a strong and delightful laugh, "What else can I get for you?"

Matthew quickly strums, *"A large Chipotle BBQ Snack Wrap, a Bacon Ranch Salad with Crispy Chicken and of course, how can I forget, your wonderful, mouthwatering McRib if you will?"*

"Okay, is there anything else?"

"Well, there is one last thing, Nancy, before I forget. If I don't order two of those Cinnamon Melts, then I might actually start to regret."

"Anything else?"

"That will be all!"

Laughing, Nancy recites, "Alright, so I have an order of a Quarter Pounder with extra fries. A large Premium Roast Coffee, two orders of the medium Chicken McBites with fries. A McCafé Mocha. A large Chipotle BBQ Snack Wrap, a Bacon Ranch Salad with Crispy Chicken and a one order of the McRibs. And finally two orders of the Cinnamon Melts. Is that correct?"

Matthew doesn't stop strumming, *"Do you have cheese on that Quarter Pounder?"*

Nancy laughs, "No I do not. Would you like me to put cheese on your Quarter Pounder?"

"Please, please, please, dear Nancy, put cheese on my Quarter Pounder for me! I would be so grateful to you!"

A short pause. And then, "Okay, your Quarter Pounder now has cheese. That will be $20.35 at the window." She then adds quickly, "Is there anything else that I can get for you?"

"Just have a wonderful afternoon, dear Nancy!"

Nancy laughs, "Thanks, you too."

"No. Thank you!" and he lightly plucks his last note.

Matthew turns to me, "Now *that* was worth listening to."

He hands me back the guitar and readjusts himself in his seat.

"Okay, excuse my language," I say, as Matthew drives up to the window where we pick up our meal. "But that was pretty fucking awesome!"

Afterward we roar off, driving and listening to the sounds of our laughter.

26

"Charlotte, could you come down here, please?" Dad calls from the living room.

I abandon my toothbrush at the side of my sink and spit out the excess toothpaste.

I skip downstairs and pause in the archway of the living room. There, Rose and Mom sit next to each other on the sofa. Rose's hands rest on her swollen belly, making me question if she had grown larger in the past weeks or if she is actually hiding a beach ball under her floral dress. Dad and Andrew stand before the low table in the living room. Andrew has traded in his Crackberry for a file folder. I look at their faces and see the seriousness in their expressions.

"Yup?" I look around from Mom to Rose, from Dad to Andrew. Everyone seems tense.

"What's wrong?" I ask. "Is this an intervention or something?"

Andrew opens his mouth to reply, but reconsiders and turns away.

Dad steps forward. "Charlotte," he says, taking my shoulder and guiding me gently to the table. "We need to talk."

"What's there to talk about?" I say. "We all already know that I have two weeks left until the big day."

"That's sort of the reason why we need to talk to you," Dad says, moving next to Andrew.

I keep my gaze on Andrew. That nauseating feeling of dislike pumps though my veins. I loathe everything about him. His slick blond hair, his towering appearance. He makes me feel smaller than I already am.

"It's about school," Dad speaks.

My hopes sail like a comet slicing across the sky. "Yes?" I eagerly ask, wondering if I will return to school sooner than what I expected.

"Your mother and I are looking for . . . special schools for you."

"What?" My head is spinning and I am utterly confused.

Did he just say, "special?"

"Wait a second. So this *is* an intervention!"

Dad, who clears his throat, says, "Charlotte, your surgery is in two weeks and we need to start preparing for the future."

Are you serious? My thoughts scream. *This can't be happening now!*

"Now, Andrew has been kind enough to do a little research for us on some of the nearby gifted schools around San Diego."

Andrew finally looks at me and opens up the folder. Inside are brochures and printed web pages of schools with names like: St. Mary's

High School for the Disabled or The San Diego School for the Gifted. The schools' titles makes them sound like they are places for non-humans. Freaks. The Wolcott High School of the Deaf. Reed's School. Madison's Gifted School.

My shoes are nailed to the floor. I can't move and I can't breathe.

Andrew speaks to me, "I personally recommend The Wolcott School." He picks up a violet brochure filled with pictures of dazed looking kids. "They really do focus on the strength of their *deaf* students."

Paralyzed, horrified, I scan the pictures. Andrew is reading out loud from the brochure, but his words never reach my ears. Instead I gag on the images of blind children being escorted by their aides, boys with twisted elbows and arms sprawled in wheelchairs. But one picture in particular stabs me straight in the heart. A girl, my age, is looking up into the sky. Her glasses are askew on the bridge of her nose. And then I notice the hearing aid attached to her ears.

I cup my hands to my mouth, holding back a scream.

Did this girl know that her picture was being taken?

Did she know what she would look like if she ever saw herself in this brochure?

Did this girl even know that she was deaf?

Did she care?

"Charlotte, are you *listening*?" I hear the irritation in Andrew's tone.

Suddenly everything becomes clear. As the eyes of my parents and my sister wait on me, I know. Right now, Rose loves Andrew because she thinks that he is trying to *help* me. Andrew is the playing the *sympathetic* and *concerned* family member who wants what's best for me. But it's a façade, and I can see clearly through it. For my parents and Rose, Andrew is picture-perfect on paper. No wonder they don't see what I see because they are blinded by the affection Andrew shares with Rose. Everything depends on Rose's happiness, and as long as Andrew makes Rose happy then my parents are happy. But standing in front of him, watching him as he proposes school after school before my own parents, I knew that I will never like Andrew as long as he is in this family. Because I now realize that this is Andrew's way of bringing his family values into our family. He is introducing what *perfection* and *the norm* would look like in the Goode family, if they got rid of the problem.

If they got rid of me.

"The hell is wrong with you?" I spit. "I'm not deaf yet, *remember*?"

"Charlotte," Rose's voice is thick. "He's just trying to help you."

"Help me? Help me!" the anger rises in my voice. "You all are getting rid of me!"

"We're not getting *rid* of you, Charlotte," Andrew murmurs. "We're trying to find a *deaf* school for you."

"Oh, screw you Andrew!" I scream.

He jumps away in shock, his eyes wide and focused on me. Both my parents shoot me dagger stares. Rose gapes at my instant rudeness.

"Charlotte!" My sister teeters to her feet.

"I'll make this job easier for all of us." I spin around and march to the coat rack; I rip my jacket off and throw open the door.

27

Norah is staring at me. I snatch a carrot from the grocery bag and slam the knife down hard on the cutting board. It makes a simple yet violent noise as I butcher the carrot rather than slice it.

I toss the remains into the sink and go for a second one.

What.

Slam.

Is.

Slam.

Wrong.

Slam.

With.

Slam.

Everybody?!

Norah, shaving the green skin off a cucumber, sits intensely in her wheelchair next to me.

This routine has been going on for a while now. I had nowhere else to go after the "intervention" my family cooked up. At least I feel like I am wanted here, with familiar walls around me. Helping Norah with her cooking keeps my mind off of the morning's blunder.   M a t t h e w observes my general discomfort from the doorway.

The two don't ask me why my eyes are swollen red from crying. They allowed me to cry in their bathroom, but neither Norah nor Matthew showers me with pity; for this I am grateful.

"Matty," Norah puts down her half shaven cucumber, "play something for us, will you?"

I pay very little attention as Matthew slips away, out of my peripheral vision.

I hack off the top of the carrot before hurling its green leaves into the sink.

"You're mad." Norah doesn't ask, but tells me.

"Yeah," I say.

"Bad day?"

"I guess you could say so."

"I have a lot of bad days too."

I find this hard to believe, since knowing Norah for the past week, she strikes me as a pleasant, chipper person.

"Some days, I wake up and hate myself because I can't do what most people can do," she tells me as she picks up her cucumber again and continues to shave it. "I sometimes feel like I'm a burden to my family. To Matthew. They give up so much for me, and they try their hardest to make life normal."

The rage leaves my body as soon as I hear the first few notes of the piano from the living room. I loosen my grip on the knife, my fingers relax as I concentrate on the notes.

"Anyway, that's why Matthew was crazy about this whole competition for *Musique Magazine*," Norah says. "He wanted his band to be represented at the MS benefit so that he could feel he was doing something for me."

The piano's tinkling tones gently pick me up, carrying me away from this world and into the hands of nothingness.

I now understand why Matthew stormed out of Brigantine when he saw Ron and me flirting with each other. He was cheated out of his opportunity. Because of me.

I try to meditate on the music. I push myself to be baptized by this musical serenity, and though I permit this sweet music to calm me, there is one sharp fragment preventing me from fully enjoying Matthew's music.

Just as the fragment sharpens, I know what it is.

I turn away from the cutting board and look toward the living room, where I see Matthew hunched over and his fingers almost airborne as he plays each of the keys on the piano. I walk past Norah and watch Matthew at his piano. Though he is ten feet away from me it feels like he's oceans away. His long brown bangs hide his eyes as he looks back and forth between his sheet music and the keys under his fingertips.

How could I not have seen it before? I had torn this boy from any hope of showing his sister that she wasn't a burden to him at all. I now know what this hideous fragment is: guilt.

I think about meeting Ron for the first time, and how he tricked me into picking him over Matthew. It's Matthew and his band who deserve to be on the cover to *Musique Magazine*, who deserve to be interviewed and who deserve to play at the magazine's benefit.

I look down to find that Norah is wheeling herself up next to me in the doorway.

Norah Lovelace . . .

It hurts me more to know just how badly I screwed up with Matthew.

Shortly, the room returns to its original silence.

Just like Matthew, I too, was given an opportunity.

But now I have certainly screwed it up for good.

Matthew's eyes meet mine.

"I wrote it just for you," he smiles.

28

On my vanity, my cell phone vibrates. I pick it up and look at the screen.

MEL, it reads.

I flip it open.

"Emergency. At office. Come now."

Click.

I don't even get a chance to open my mouth as Mel's panicked voice booms into my ear.

I march out of the elevator and into the office.

"Oh Charlotte!" Mel dramatically raises her voice as soon as she sees me. "We have a problem!"

"What?" I walk beside Mel, ignoring how the office has been transformed into a top-notch photo shoot. Orange and black wires are rolled on the carpet and light bulbs explode from the photographers.

"One of the Bond Boys broke his wrist."

"Come again?"

I stop.

"Which one?" I ask.

"The guitar player, Cole Winebread." She turns away from me and continues to walk down the hallway to the conference room. "But that's the least of our problems."

"The least of our problems? The dude broke his wrist!"

"I'm *aware* of that."

"Well then, how did he break it?"

Mel stops in front of the conference room. She releases a low sigh and answers, "Because of this—"

She throws open the doors to the conference room.

"This has gone far enough!" The platinum blond Ty Shrew shouts at Ron. "I'm sick of you acting like you're the next Paul McCarthy!"

He shoves his albino fingers at Ron's chest.

"I'm acting? I'm acting? Without me, Blondie, we wouldn't have gotten this job in the first place!" Ron smacks Ty's finger away and shoves him violently in the shoulders.

Ty nearly falls to the floor, until his twin brother, Nick, steps in.

"Back off, okay!" Nick firmly holds onto his brother. "This is enough! I mean look what you did to Cole!"

"It was his own fault," Ron folds his arms over his chest. "He tried to punch me and I simply just moved out of his way."

"Yeah. But that also caused him to shatter his wrist against the wall, you dumbass!" Nick's face morphs to a bright red. "And that was only because he wanted to try something different but you wouldn't allow him to go out of line!"

I crane my neck in the doorway and see Cole sitting on the couch with an ice brace and a cloth wrapped around his wrist. His shoulders are shaking and his eyes are puffy.

"He wanted to be the lead singer for one of the songs."

"Oh my God, Ron!" Ty speaks into Ron's face. "It's one stupid song, why do you care so much?"

Weeks ago, I would have run up and comforted Ron. I would have calmed him down or hugged him, to stop his anger from controlling him.

But I don't. I am just like the rest of the witnesses in this office. The Charlotte who swooned for Ron weeks ago would have taken him outside to cool down and listen to him rant about his frustrations. But that's not me anymore.

As I watch this all play out, I now secretly wish that Matthew was here.

It was like a trap. That guilty feeling sweeps me back into the unforgiving current.

This should be Lennox, my thoughts are clear as day. It is obvious that Matthew and his band should be in this conference room instead of the Bond Boys.

And from the way the Bond Boys are acting I allow a glimmer of hope to slither into my thoughts.

If the Bond Boys are fighting, then that means that they've split. Which means Mel will have to look for a new band!

I am so confident in my hypothesis that I turn to Mel and say, "Well I guess that's the end. After a fight like this, there's no way that this band will ever get back together. Should I ask Lennox if they are still interested in playing for the benefit?"

Mel eyes me, "What the hell are you talking about? We're not replacing this band! We have to pull them together."

I am confused by her response, "Pull them together?"

"Exactly."

"But, they're fighting. They're obviously going to split."

"Not yet," she says coldly. "We still have time to smooth things over with them. We have to make sure that they don't split until the benefit."

So Mel wasn't going to get rid of them?

"But, how are they going to play without their guitarist?"

"We'll figure something out," Mel says. "Right, Charlotte?"

Whenever Mel uses the word "we" in one of her maestro sentences, it usually translates to:

You need to smooth things over with them, Charlotte.

You figure something out.

But how can I figure out anything if all I can think of is Matthew?

29

It had ended up being a very odd day. After I left Mel's office, it felt like I was carrying a pot of acid and had to be careful not to spill it all over the place until the end of the day. Which is why I now call Matthew and walk over to his house. I tell him that we need to discuss something very important.

"Door's open!" I hear Matthew's voice as I step through the threshold of his home and find him sprawled on the couch, guitar on his lap, playing an acoustic version of one of his songs.

I walk over to him and stand by the side of the couch.

"Hey," he says.

"Hey," I answer.

I remember locking myself in the conference room with a bunch of pissed off boys after Mel had left. I scolded them, telling them that they were nothing but arrogant little boys who didn't know how the hell to share. And finally, when everyone's nerves were calmed down, I proposed my idea to the Bond Boys about their guitarist. Obviously, poor Cole Winebread with his shattered wrist couldn't even pick up his guitar. If the Bond Boys were to stay focused until the benefit, then adjustments had to be made. I wonder how I got through the day without regretting the decision that I made with Ron and his two remaining band members. I was beginning to believe that it was because I had Matthew all curled up in the back of my thoughts. It wasn't just because I was always happy to see him or that he was always happy to see me. It was because Matthew was just plain, gangly, clumsy Matthew. Yes, he was the exact opposite of Ron. He was never confident or uptight; he was reserved and sweet. However, doubting his confidence in almost everything, when Matthew opens his mouth to sing or strums his guitar, it's as if he's created a whole new world around himself.

"So, what's the emergency?" he sits up, adjusting the guitar strings.

"Mel called me," I say.

I make sure that my sentences are short as I tell Matthew about the Bond Boys and their violent quarrel.

"Oh, wow," Matthew's hairy eyebrows wiggle over his eyes. "So you talked to them."

"Yeah."

"I guess they've lost a member of their band."

"Yup. Which is why I recommended you," the words suddenly leave my mouth.

"You *what*?" Matthew flips his guitar off of his lap.

The acid that I was carrying before now suddenly tips over. I wait for the burning to begin.

"Why the hell did you do that?"

"Because they need a guitarist to play with them at the benefit."

"Yeah. But why me, Charlotte?"

Because I made the biggest mistake by choosing Ron's band over your band, and I'm really, really sorry for doing that.

I don't say those exact words to him out loud.

"Because," I scratch my head, "You deserve it."

"But, Ron could not have allowed this."

"Oh, he allowed it."

Okay, that is a lie. When I met with the Bond Boys, I told them that I knew a guitarist who could replace Cole. But I didn't say who, only that he was a good guitarist who was fast enough to pick up on beats. Nick and Ty seemed really grateful that I found a solution to their band's predicament, but Ron's response on the other hand was mainly passive before he waved me off. My fear was that if I had said Matthew's name, Ron wouldn't be onboard with the rest of his band.

"But what about *my* band, Charlotte? How are Xander and Jeremiah going to feel when they hear that I'm joining forces with our competing band?"

"This isn't about Xander or Jeremiah, or even about Ron, Matthew," I say, my heart knocking against my rib cage.

Matthew draws himself up and drops his face into the palms of his hands.

"Besides," I add softly. "it should have been you all along."

After a moment of hesitation, I watch Matthew lift his head from his hands.

"Alright," he says. "When do I come in?"

30

In the elevator, my heart feels like it is being squeezed like a stress ball, and I can't stop my fingers from twitching against my jeans.

"Hey," Matthew says next to me. "Are you okay?"

I whip my head around. His guitar bag hangs over his right shoulder.

"Yup," I lie, as I pinch a piece of my flesh between my fingers.

"It's okay," Matthew claps my back, a huge grin moving across his rosy cheeks. "After watching Ron and his band playing at Crown Records all this month, I know that they can seem intimidating at times. You, of course, already know that."

If only that was the only thing to worry about, I think.

So far, I have managed to cover the first step of my plan by convincing Matthew to unite with Ron and his two remaining band members. Now it is time for the final phase of my plan. I told myself that this was going to work, but the more I pretended that everything was going to be fine, the jitterier I felt.

I cross my fingers behind my back. When the doors slide open, I walk out first, with Matthew following behind me.

There's no sign of yesterday's disastrous photo shoot.

"You work here?" I hear Matthew gasp at the band posters and framed magazine covers.

"*Used* to work," I correct him.

Slips of sounds come from underneath the doors to the conference room.

"This way," I direct him down the hall.

I rest my hands on the twin knobs, but I don't open them just yet.

"Ready?" I ask him.

"Ready."

I'm not, but I turn the knobs anyway and swing open the doors.

Ron, Nick and Ty are adjusting their instruments. Cords sprawl across the floor and the drum set is assembled and pushed against the back wall. Ron's head is down as he picks at the strings of his Vox while Nick helps his brother adjust the drum's cymbals.

Mel has her back to us, but then pivots around in a skirt seemingly glued to her thighs and a ruffled blouse that makes her look like a nineteenth century gothic.

"Oh, Charlotte!" she presses her hands together and walks up to Matthew and me. "I knew I could count on you to solve this little bump for the benefit."

Her amber eyes grow into slits as she closely examines Matthew.

"And you must be—"

"Matthew Lovelace from Lennox."

The low musical adjustments stop all together in the background.

"Very well. I'm sure you have a lot to catch up on with your new band so I'll leave you to be better acquainted," Mel says, scanning her eyes one more time down Matthew's clothes. "In the meantime, I'll be down at Starbucks editing some papers. Excuse me."

She pushes through us and out of the conference room. Once we hear the soft click of the doors, we find ourselves in the middle of a hungry pack of wolves. But the final installment to my plan was in effect: Ron and Matthew are now together in one place.

Slowly, Matthew and I turn to the Bond Boys, who stare at us quizzically.

Ron is the first to pounce.

"What is *he* doing here?" Ron's apple green eyes dart between Matthew and me and then quickly to the guitar bag on Matthew's shoulder.

Out of the corner of my eye, I see Matthew spin directly in front of me.

"You didn't tell *him*?"

His fists are clenched at his sides, and his face is red with anger and embarrassment.

"Tell *him*?" Ron shoots back. "Tell him *what* exactly?"

Both boys glare at me and I feel the sweat prickling at my forehead.

First I turn to Ron, inhaling air until my lungs feel like a pair of inflated balloons. "You needed a new band member," I say, placing my hands on my hips. "After what happened with Cole and his wrist, you need another guitarist."

"Yeah," Ron hisses at me like it should have been obvious. "But I thought we agreed on someone *new*, not someone like *Matthew*."

"Well, he's the best guitarist I know and I doubt that he will be a disappointment."

Matthew adverts his eyes to the floor.

"He stays," says I. "That's final."

Now to Matthew. "And you," I address him. He raises his brown eyes, "You deserve this."

"Charlotte—" he rolls his eyes up to the ceiling.

"No. No, stop it okay," I slam my fist into the palm of my hand. "I know you. I know you can do this. And I most certainly know that this is what you want."

Everyone goes quiet, their eyes looking around the room.

"We have an extra amp here," Ty Shrew points to an amp in the corner of the conference room. "You can plug in your guitar when you're ready."

Ron snarls as Matthew takes one last look at me and walks over to join the Bond Boys.

31

Matthew is pissed off.

I can tell by the way his fingers angrily slice through the cords of his guitar. Matthew's strumming changes quickly from tolerable to, finally, impatient.

Nick and Ty seem to be picking up the same agitated waves. I've been here in this conference room for two full hours. I *was* hoping to go over the paperwork, finalize the details for the benefit, but I keep re-reading the same paragraph. Ron is giving shit to Matthew about the way he is holding his guitar or how offbeat he is.

This really pokes at me.

I want to go up to Ron and be all like, "Shut the fuck up, dude! At least he's trying."

But that's the problem. Matthew himself isn't even trying. After rehearsing one of the Bond Boys' songs for ten minutes—and then being yelled at by Ron for not following the band's lead—I can tell that Matthew has already given up trying to please Ron.

Insert the Apocalypse here.

Ron then wastes—I don't know—15 to 20 minutes accusing Matthew of purposely ruining his gig.

It's bearable to listen to Ron when he yells at Matthew, because most of the time, Matthew just lets Ron waylay him with his words without talking back to him. But when it's Ron *and* Matthew arguing with each other, it feels like the entire building is shaking. But *then*, when it's Ron, Matthew *and* Nick and Ty, the universe collapses into a huge black hole of arguments, curses and profanities.

What's worse, I'm getting a headache from listening to this band argue. And since I'm getting nothing accomplished, I've now started timing the arguments to prepare myself for when the next nuclear weapon will be launched.

Like right now . . .

"The fuck was that?!" Ron growls.

"What?"

"What do you mean, what?"

I sigh for the twentieth (yes I'm counting) time today. I rub my eyes and advert my gaze away from the documents I'm reading for the benefit's venue.

Ron stares at Matthew, his eyes tense and angry. "That thing you do on your guitar that you call *strumming* is an embarrassment not only to the song but to me."

Where's Mel? I never imagined myself asking that question before, picturing Mel as my hero of the day. But then I remember: *Oh right, she's editing papers downstairs at Starbucks.*

"Oh, I'm so sorry then," I hear the sarcasm in Matthew's voice rise.

Don't take the bait. Don't take the bait. Don't take the bait, I repeat over in my head for Matthew's sake.

"Maybe this is more to your liking . . ."

So Matthew bends down and spins the dial on the amp before ripping his fingers through his strings, contaminating the room with an awful off–pitched shrill.

"That better for you, now?"

"You guys quit it!" Nick demands.

"Please . . ." I whisper, messaging my temples.

Again, a tsunami of pain crashes against my cranium.

"Ron. Mat. Let's forget it okay," says Ty. "It's five o'clock already and we haven't fully practiced one song yet!"

However, Ron and Matthew ignore the twin's pleas and go at it again.

My jaw tightens as Ron lashes back at Matthew with some sour remark.

As I sit here listening, the twins begin to argue with Matthew and Ron, and the world comes crashing down.

The sounds burn my eardrums.

You guys, please stop it.

The arguments start to fly by fast, like a reflex.

They yell.

They snap.

They growl.

The insults they produce are scrutinizing.

"SHUT UP!" a voice screams.

My voice.

My screams.

The silence greets me again.

The Bond Boys and Matthew look at me in disbelief.

"JUST SHUT THE FUCK UP!"

I am unable to move from where I stand.

Only now do I realize that I am standing.

When did I stand up?

I stare at the little band. They look too tired and shocked to do anything at the moment. But now, there is no sound of voices. No words of insult and no noise.

I have to leave.

I pick up my coat and, without looking twice, walk out the door and into the silent night.

32

As if this night couldn't get any worse.

I walk all the way from work to my house, exercising the anger out of me.

But when I climb the steps to the porch, my ears ache with Rose and Andrew's own quarrel.

"I just think you should have told me before you popped the question to her," says Andrew.

"Why are you making this such a big deal?" Rose replies.

I can see the two standing before the sink . . . talking about me.

"Because it's Charlotte . . ."

"Yeah. My sister, remember?"

"No! I mean it's Charlotte with a *problem*."

"So what then?" Rose. "Should I call Charlotte and tell her that one of *your* sisters would make a better godmother than her? I mean, how do you think she's going to feel?"

"Well, what are *you* going to do then, Rose?" Andrew. "She's deaf!"

That's when I finally get enough.

I walk in, and stand in the kitchen doorway. There I face the silent, sullen faces of my sister and my brother–in–law.

I look directly at Andrew, "Get out."

I am getting sick from the ugliness in my own voice.

Andrew doesn't move.

I turn to the kitchen table where his coat and car keys lie.

I tear his coat off the back of the chair and crumble it into a medium-sized ball.

"NOW!"

I fling the coat at his chest. The keys fall short of his shoes.

Andrew is silent. He looks at Rose before bending down to swipe his keys off the floor. He doesn't meet my eyes as he passes me and slams the door behind him.

I look up at Rose. Her face is whiter than salt.

"How could you!" Rose says to me. "How—"

But her voice cracks into a sob.

She can't finish her sentence.

As soon as Andrew leaves, my parents rush downstairs to ask what all the shouting was about.

Rose wails to my parents what happened. How she and Andrew got into an stupid argument over who should be the baby's godmother and how I walked in and screamed at Andrew to leave.

Both my parents' eyes fall on me. They guide me to the couch. By this time, my legs feel like lead as I walk to the living room, where my parents give me a good scolding about respecting people under our roof.

But I am tired, and the painful throbbing in my head pulses every time either Mom or Dad raise their voices at me.

It sucks in so many ways.

My head is too crazy; the thoughts bounce around inside my skull like a swarm of angry bees.

Noisy.

Ugly.

"Do you understand me, Charlotte?" It's Mom's voice bringing me back to reality.

To be honest, I tuned out my parents' anger at me as soon as I slumped against the cushions of the couch.

I shrug, "Sure."

Then they all leave me. Rose retires to the guest bedroom alone, without Andrew tonight. And my mom and dad split off into their separate rooms. Mom to the bedroom, to finish watching whatever soap opera is on at night. And Dad to his office, to finish writing his deposition.

I am all alone, on the couch.

Only the hatred and pain from the noises that I've heard today accompany me.

Pain so bad that I consider death with a handshake or smile, just to be free from it.

To be deaf from it.

Deafness.

I look up at the flight of stairs, where Dad's office door is open.

It's all noise, I think. *So why am I fighting so hard to keep it?*

33

The walls of Dad's office are almost prison-like.

When I was younger, I used to call his office the dungeon. Hence the fact that he had no windows and, although very bad for his eyesight, he preferred to leave the overhead lights off and work just by the light of his desk lamp.

Dad sits at his desk in a rickety, old, wooden chair. The yellow light of his desk lamp pools over the screen of his computer, where he is typing away.

I stand next to him. He raises his eyes up at me.

"What is it, Charlotte?" he asks gruffly. He was the most mad at me when I threw Andrew out of the house.

"I just needed some quiet time. From Andrew, from everyone." I halfheartedly explain.

"I see."

"Dad."

"Yeah?"

I twist my eyes away from my hands and back up at him.

"The surgery," I say. "I only have a week left."

"Okay," Dad fully turns in his chair to face me. "What about it?"

I let my hands fall to my sides, "I don't want the surgery in a week."

I stand very still, while Dad's eyes fix on my face in confusion.

The silence lengthens, and Dad's features are immobile as stone.

"I think I'm ready now," I say to him.

Dad's blank expression tells me how sudden my decision is.

His eyes zero in on me.

"Charlotte," Dad's voice is softer. "Is this what you really want?"

I recall my serious problems.

It seems like if I have the surgery sooner my life will be less miserable without the awful sounds following me wherever I go.

Deafness is the answer.

"Yes," I draw a deep breath.

Dad replies with a heavy sigh.

"I'll call Dr. Days," he says. "I'll ask her for the soonest appointment for your surgery."

I nod understandingly.

I square my shoulders and walk out of Dad's office, trudging back downstairs to play my violin, one last time.

34

As soon as I adjust the strings on my violin, I hear Dad coming downstairs. He stops at the landing and looks at me.

"I called Dr. Days," he says slowly to me. "She says that she will take you in Saturday morning for your surgery."

Nothing more is said, as I hear his footsteps returning back upstairs to his office.

I play in the dark.

The Mozart piece flows out of me like never before, like my fingers have become part of the strings and bow.

My fingers shake from pressing down on the strings too hard.

After years of walking with Lexi to the recording studio, I'd grown an attachment to the dark cherry-wood violin in Mr. Abbot's musical closet. I had wandered over there after getting tired of playing the bongos for an hour and wanted to try out something else. Then I saw it in its case.

The violin, cradled against the velvet—it almost looked like a baby to me. And as I kept staring at its polished wood and thin bow, I could have sworn that it was begging me to hold it. Not even hold it, but touch it. Play it.

It's been almost nine years now.

I think I will miss the violin sound the most. Because it speaks to me.

I am concentrating on the last note of my piece when the phone shrieks.

"Death row, how can I help you?" I answer the phone impassively.

"Charlotte?" Lexi's voice answers. "Hey, what's up? You wanna grab some breakfast tomorrow? Clayton's Coffee Shop is having a sale on their famous flapjacks from eight to ten."

I stand, mute.

"Charlotte?"

"Yeah, I'm here."

"Is everything okay?"

Mute again.

Suddenly, I can't see. My eyes sting with tears.

"Lexi," I walk over to the doorframe and lean my forehead against the chipped wood of the archway.

"I'm having the surgery Saturday," I sigh.

"Saturday?" Lexi sounds confused. "But that's the day after tomorrow."

There is a beat of silence.

"That's crazy, Charlotte," Lexi says. "You're supposed to have a week left."

"I changed the date."

"Why?"

"Because they hurt my ears."

"Who's 'they,' Charlotte?"

"Ron," I manage to say out loud. "And Matthew and Rose and Andrew."

"Matthew?" Lexi sounds shocked. "What did he do to you?"

"He yelled."

"At you?"

"At Ron. And Ron yelled back at him and the twins started yelling at both of them and then when I got home Rose and Andrew were arguing and I yelled at them and now my head hurts and my ears hurt and all I want is silence," I sob. "Try and understand, Lexi."

But she doesn't respond.

"Lexi. Lexi?"

There's no one on the other end.

SATURDAY

Tomorrow!

I finally get out tomorrow!

Ready for the big day? Nurse Frizzy asks me, bringing me a cup of water as I sit up in my bed.

I nod.

Take one last walk around the place, Nurse Frizzy signs. *You'll need all the strength in your muscles to walk out of these doors.*

She's right.

And besides, I need to stop and say goodbye to someone.

I knock on Cancer Kid's door.

He raises his head up from his pillow to see me.

His eyes are swollen, and the tubes are still connected to his tiny body.

"May I come in?" I ask.

Cancer Kid nods.

I teeter into his room, with the violin case in my hand.

Instantly, Cancer Kid sits up when he sees me walk in with the case.

I rest the case on one of the chairs, and slowly unclip the locks, where my beautiful violin greets me from its velvet bed.

Now Cancer Kid watches me tune the strings.

'Course, I can't tell if the tune is right or not because of the obvious.

I slide out my bow.

"I apologize if my notes are a bit off," I say to Cancer Kid even though I can't hear my own voice.

He doesn't move; his eyes are glued on me and my violin.

I swing my violin to my chin and I rest my bow above the first string. My shoulder supports the violin as I glance up at Cancer Kid.

I take a stab in the dark.

I feel the music in my fingers. The vibrations under each string correspond correctly to my memory of the Mozart piece I am playing. I dip my bow to one side to begin the melody again. I can see each note before my eyes.

I slide my bow down to what I feel is the correct high note. I can almost feel the air become tinted with the sensation of sound.

My fingers ache as I clutch the neck of my violin, but I continued to play, this time with more power as I swoon and tip my bow in different directions.

I concentrate on each note, and the hum against my cheek.

Finally, I curve my bow sideways and slowly hit the final note.

I pull my bow away from my violin and look directly at Cancer Kid.

His eyes are wide and he opens his lips.

Beautiful, he mouths to me before breaking into applause.

35

It's morning.

My last morning.

As I lie awake in my bed I concentrate on the cries of the seagulls and the low rustling of the trees outside my window.

This will all be gone by tomorrow, I think.

The springs under my mattress squeak.

The clock in my room ticks like a heartbeat.

My radio hums . . .

Wait.

I sit upright and look around my room.

I don't own a radio.

I tear the sheets off my bed and walk to my dresser where my iPod sits.

I pick it up.

The screen is dark.

I hear the collapse and explosion of drums coming from outside.

Outside?

I turn to my window, which overlooks the front lawn.

Unbelievable.

I throw open the windows and the shock of music fills my room.

Standing on my lawn are Matthew, Lexi and the Bond Boys, along with their instruments.

The electrified beats continue as Nick pounds on his drums and Ty's fingers dance across the keys of his keyboard. But it is the sight of Ron and Matthew that makes the song more beautiful. Ron, as always, cuts his fingers across his Vox, and Matthew, standing next to him, sings as loudly as his voice will go while his fingers pluck away.

I see Lexi, standing next to the black Toyota in the driveway, waving at me.

Immediately, I wave back.

Thank you, I mouth to her.

It sounds like someone has placed a ginormous set of Bose headphones around the walls of my room and cranked up the volume.

The glorious, wonderful music has returned to me, extinguishing the painful noises from last night.

The sounds swallow me and finally heal me.

Matthew finishes off his guitar solo with a low thud and all four of them shoot their heads up at me.

"How was that?" Matthew asks.

I clap.

"That was killer! Oh my God!" I shout back to him.

"So, I take it that you'll hold off on the surgery then?" Ron asks.

I pull my head out from the window and frown.

Ron fixes his apple green eyes on me. "Lexi filled me in."

Lexi raises another eyebrow at Ron who rolls his eyes away from her and back up to me.

"And she wanted me to apologize to you for fighting with Matthew and the band."

"Apology accepted," I answer.

"So . . ." Matthew walks closer under my window. "You're gonna wait?"

I look down at the band for a second before I slam my window shut.

I run to my closet, where I slip on a pair of shoes and drape my coat over my pajama top. I run through my room and down stairs. I throw open the front door and speed past the band outside on my lawn.

"Charlotte!" I hear Matthew's voice calling me as I tear down the street. "Where are you going?"

I don't have time to answer.

I keep running.

36

She knows I'm here, but she's not acknowledging me.

When I arrived at Dr. Days' house—six or seven blocks away from my own house—Aunt Kilda had answered the door. When I asked her where Dr. Days was, she directed me to the back of the house, where I found Dr. Days gardening.

I didn't even know that she liked flowers.

"I was wondering if you could help me with this, Charlotte," Dr. Days says without taking her eyes off her rose bush.

I thought she meant the flowers, but Dr. Days makes no attempt to hand me any gardening tools to help her cut her roses.

In fact, her back is still turned.

"Um . . . sure," I look around Dr. Days' garden. "What do you need?"

"Well," her pliers snip at the throat of one of her roses. "Tell me. What should one do when they get personally invested in someone?"

223

What did she just ask me?

I don't answer. I'm hanging on her question when she spins around to face me, three roses in her gloved hands.

"I think I can guess why you are here," she says rather coldly to me.

She darts her robin-egg blue eyes at me like I am some determined target that upsets her.

"I made a mistake."

"Don't we all."

"I take it my Dad called you about the surgery."

"The earliest slot that I could offer him is tomorrow."

"About that—" I say, hoping that it is obvious to her that I wasn't myself last night and made the wrong call at the wrong time.

"I have a lot on my mind right now," Dr. Days interrupts me as she spins back to her roses. "Gardening usually helps me organize my thoughts."

No kidding. I remind myself to be calm.

"If it's not too much to ask," I take one step closer next to her. "Can I have my original date back?"

Dr. Days ignores me and continues working with her flowers.

I can't believe Dr. Days is blowing me off! Can't she understand what I've been through? What my entire month had ended up being and how having the surgery sooner would only make things worse for me? My wish would be granted; I would be deaf by tomorrow.

I turn to leave.

"I am disappointed in you, Charlotte," Dr. Days says smoothly.

I am puzzled by her comment and I turn to face her back.

"Disappointed?" my tensions rise. "Why? Why me?"

I see her expression grow harsh and bitter.

"Because I have a hard job, Charlotte!" she raises her voice at me.

"Oh. So you're taking your anger out on me this time, right?"

"No!" she yanks another rose from her bush. "I'm an oncologist, Charlotte. What do you think my day consists of? Smiley faces and rainbows? No!

"My entire day is filled with children younger than you, dying! And then having to watch the parents of those children suffer, asking me why I couldn't save their baby. Well, I've tried saving as many patients as I could, Charlotte! Sometimes I succeed but mostly I don't. And every time I don't succeed, I ask myself why *she* died or why *he* died and what I didn't do to save them!"

I am dumbstruck. Never have I realized what someone like Dr. Days goes through in her everyday life. Let alone, this is her job, confronting and challenging cancer until the bitter end.

"From the moment that I met you, Charlotte, I knew that you were something. Your disease was quite extraordinary at the time, and I was fascinated yet horrified how you inherited this disease. And I guess in all fairness, I sort of grew attached to you. Though, at the time I kept a distance just in case something awful happened to you –"

"Like I would die?" I cross my arms.

"In a sense, yes," she answers while she snips. "But when I saw the brain scan and the tumors, I saw an opportunity."

"An opportunity?" I rub the back of my skull. "No offense, but having two tumors growing inside your brain wouldn't exactly qualify as an *opportunity*."

"Well, for me Charlotte, it was." She adds two more roses to her bouquet. "I saw it as a chance for me to save a life."

I remember at the beginning of the month sitting in Dr. Days' office listening to her and my family about my probable deafness. While I looked at it as the death of my hearing, Dr. Days saw it as her chance to save my life.

"And because I was struck with the realization that I could help you get through this disease, I used it as a sort of excuse to develop an attachment to you. And that's where the sign language lessons came in."

Another snip. Another rose.

"So over the past month, Charlotte, I've become personally invested in you. But as time went on, I knew that I had made a mistake."

"A mistake?"

For a moment I think the ground under me shifts. Though, I didn't realize that this was how Dr. Days felt about me. I am surprised that her conclusion about me ends on a negative note.

"Last night, when I got the call from your dad, Charlotte, medically I knew that having the surgery sooner was good for you." She says. "After the seizure, I thought that I failed another patient."

I feel the ice being injected into my veins.

"But . . ." she lowers her pliers and her roses, her eyes looking down to the earth. "When I heard you play your violin that one morning in front of Kilda, I—" She pauses and turns to face me. "I heard something that I never heard before in my life. I heard . . . passion. Pure passion."

I stand motionless. Out of everyone who has ever heard me play my violin, not one person has told me that they detected any emotion.

"That's when I knew. Not only was I going to save your life, but I was stealing something from you too. I was stealing away something that you loved most. I should be happy that your Dad told me that you wanted the surgery sooner," Dr. Days detaches her gaze away from mine. "But I'm not."

I am frozen. After all these years of acting like a total bitch to Dr. Days, it was her all along who was watching over me, who cared enough to spend the entire month with me so that I could live out my life as normally as possible once I'm deaf. She understood more than anyone else what I am going through and was simply trying to help me. She understood my pain. And the consequence of saving my life was to take away something that I loved dearly. In order to live, I have to give up my hearing. And Dr. Days realized this difficult decision.

Nevertheless, she *wanted* me to live.

"So, what should I do?" I ask her. "What should I do now that I still have my hearing?"

Dr. Days takes one step closer to me.

"Use this time to listen, Charlotte."

That doesn't seem to help when all this time I've been listening to my iPod, Matthew, Ron and the band.

"I'll give you the original day back," she slides a rose out from the bunch in her hands and begins cutting off the sharp tips of the thorns. "But I suggest that maybe if you're going to keep your hearing you should probably listen to your parents."

She then hands me the thornless rose.

"Because they might have something to say."

37

As I walk back to the house, rose in my hand, I begin to think about my parents. Mainly my mom.

Other than being known only for her obsession with me and running around the island at the crack of dawn *and* always smelling of Olay Age Defying Cream *and* having a strong Boston accent, she is the strongest human being I know.

When it was made known to her friends that I was screwed, people started to ask frequently how I was doing. Whenever the neighbors came by to bring their cooked casseroles and get well soon cards, my mom always stared-slit-eyed while they looked at my bandages from the doorway.

Whenever we come home from the hospital, our neighbor who always waters her lawn would watch as Dad unloads me from the car. But it was my mom who would shoot the woman the "what-are-you-look-ing-at?" stare before the neighbor would realize that she had drowned her prized chrysanthemums in water.

Even the round, stony face of my mom could leak out some sort of hidden emotion. She saw the tremor in me, but over the years she had been getting good at paving away the cracks and holes in her expressions.

The front lawn is deserted when I come home and see my mom and dad in the kitchen.

They ask me where I've been and why there was a boy band playing rock 'n' roll music under my window.

I guess my parents shooed them away, as there is no trace of Nick's drum set, Ty's keyboard or even Matthew, Ron and Lexi anywhere in front of the house.

"That was the band that I picked for the benefit," I explain. "Lexi brought them over to try to cheer me up. As for me, I went to Dr. Days' house," I reply, twirling the rose in between my thumb and forefinger.

"Charlotte," my Mom looks at me stiffly. "What were you doing there?"

I tell her how I asked Dr. Days to give me back my week of hearing.

"Why the hell did you do that, Charlotte?"

I thought she meant talking to Dr. Days about having my original day back for the surgery. This hurts me a bit. I didn't know that Mom agreed with Dr. Days' first view that having the surgery sooner might be best for me.

But then she says, "Why would you want to have the surgery tomorrow?"

I explain to her about the events of the last few days that drove me to produce the idea that deafness was the only way out of this world.

"That's outrageous, Charlotte!" Mom grasps the edge of the sink. "That and kicking your own brother-in-law out of the house. Do you have any idea how devastated your sister is? She won't even come out of her old bedroom!"

I don't answer, because I know that throwing Andrew out of the house was the wrong thing to do. But I won't lie to myself, I still don't like him.

"Damnit, Charlotte, I am sick of you doing what you think is right for yourself!"

I stay quiet.

I just listen.

"Do you know what you've been acting like over the past few weeks?"

I shake my head, listening.

"You've been acting selfish, Charlotte! Completely selfish!"

Selfish, I repeat the word in my head. *That seems to fit just right.*

"I agree with your mother," Dad says, lowering his head but then looking up at me.

"When you told me what you wanted to do, you didn't even consider what *we*, your family, must be thinking of your behavior. Rose is crying right now, about the inappropriate character that you displayed before her and Andrew."

They keep talking.

I keep listening.

But when two hours go by, the message is clear: I have been a selfish brat before my family.

I didn't even think about my parents' pain while I spent my time at Matthew's house, or with Mel in her office or even with Lexi.

"Do you understand now, Charlotte?" my mom crosses her arms over her chest. "Do you have anything to say?"

I do. I look at the rose, still alive and red in my hands.

I look up at my mom and hand the rose to her.

"I'm sorry, you guys," I tell my parents after Mom has taken the rose. "You have no idea just how sorry I am."

38

Rose is in her old room.

I knock on the door.

"Go away," I hear her hiss, putting in as much poison into her whisper as she can.

"I came to apologize."

She doesn't respond, and I take it as an invitation to walk in.

Rose is sitting on her comforter, which had been stripped away from its original pink sheets when she went to college. We now use her old room as a second storage facility in addition to the garage.

She is wearing a floral dress and is resting her arms over her round belly.

"Close the door," she orders me, like this is still her room.

I do so, before cupping my hands in the back pockets of my pajamas.

"What do you want?" she lightly sobs.

"I came here to listen," I whisper anxiously.

"To what?"

"To whatever you need to say."

"Look, Charlotte," her voice is nearly soundless. "I love you, so much. And that was the only reason Andrew and I drove down here, to support you in your time of need." She speaks slowly, making each word distinct. "But what you did to me, to Andrew, was unforgivable."

I exhale deeply, struggling with the effect of Rose's words.

Unforgivable. Will that be the last word that I hear from Rose?

I take in Rose's blank expression and watch as her eyes swiftly turn to a box stacked up with photo albums. She is gazing at one in particular. A white photo album with the cover framing Rose and Andrew's wedding picture.

A frown dominates the beautiful face of my sister as she stares at the photo album, and I know what she is thinking.

Andrew . . .

The man whom Rose had cried in her sleep for when she was only a junior in college. The harsh relationship they had as friends and as a couple. But the happiness that she had found when he proposed to her, married her and is now having a child with her.

I watch Rose as she rubs the tears off her checks.

What was it about perky Rose and rude Andrew that made them such a good couple? How can two people with different ways of approaching life come to love each other so much that they have a baby together? Was I missing something from this equation?

Wonderful, nice, beautiful, popular Rose. How come she didn't marry someone like her, but ended up marrying someone the exact opposite of her? Is the saying true? That opposites do attract?

I'm not Rose and I don't live in her head, but what is life like with Andrew that seems to bring her happiness every day? There was very little display of affection that I saw between the two when they stayed over. Then again, I wasn't at home most of the time to see Rose and Andrew together. So who am I to make judgments?

Did they go on walks when I was at Matthew's house? Did he kiss her at all when I was not around?

But my point being: what did it matter if I hated Andrew with all my guts? Andrew is just one guy out of the thousands of other people who still like me. But it was Rose whom he truly loved out of anyone in the entire world.

Selfish, my mom's words remind me.

She is right. What I did to Rose was selfish.

"Rose," I walk over to the bed and sit down next to her. I put a hand on her back and say to her, "Go home."

"Excuse me?"

"Rose," I breathe. "Go home."

Rose sucks in a startled breath and then pushes herself up from the comforter and looks down to face me. "What do you mean?"

"I mean, ask Mom to drive you down to the train station and call Andrew to pick you up there in an hour."

Her face turns tense again with effort, "But what about you?"

"I'll be fine," I say, my cheeks growing warm. "But right now what *you* need is your husband."

"Charlotte," Rose closes her eyes and opens them again. "I can't just waltz out of here when the day of your surgery is so close."

I make a weak grimace.

I don't want Rose to leave, but for her benefit and for Andrew's and the baby's, it is a requirement.

"Sure you can," I take her hand. "Because Andrew did it. Why can't you?"

"Charlotte—"

"Andrew needs you, Rose." Rose's face softens when I say her husband's name. "Just call me when you get off the train safely."

Rose pulls me up from the comforter by my hand, and I suddenly thud against her belly. She embraces me and rubs my hair while the baby bump between us feels like it is about to crush my ribs.

"You're awesome, you know that?" she mutters against my hair.

"Rose—" I gasp. "I can't breathe!"

She releases me at once, her hands still around my waist.

"Sorry," she chuckles uneasily. "I should get packing."

39

Almost everything is back to normal.

The post apocalyptic normal, that is.

When Mom drove Rose and me to the train station to see her off, the last words she said to me were, "She will love you."

"She?"

"My daughter."

And then she boarded the train and was gone.

After Rose's departure, I am once again the center of my parents' attention. Mom goes back to complaining that my hair looks terrible. And after the sixth or so complaint, I call up Lexi and we schedule an appointment at the hair salon to get my hair shortened for the surgery. When I return home with a pixie haircut, there is little that my mom could say. Dad follows me everywhere I go. Though there are some advantages of having your mid-forty-ish father join you on walks to Spreckles Park or on the beach, (such as buying me ice cream). Can't really see anything bad about that.

I call Matthew and ask him if his family would join mine for dinner. I even add a yes, Norah can make something to bring to the house, just as long as it isn't too much.

When Matthew, Norah and his parents arrive, they bring more food than I expected. They each ornament the table with a main dish, relieving my mom of her duty as chef for the evening.

Matthew gives me a hug, complimenting my new haircut before setting down a large bowl of steamed vegetables. He is wearing his black leather jacket once again. Norah rolls in, looking amazing in a coral pink dress with her hair pinned in a bun.

The house smells delicious.

Dad turns on the radio in the kitchen to some classical station.

"Sorry for the food overload," Matthew says, pulling out the chair next to me. "You can blame it on Norah, of course."

Norah rolls her chair in between her parents, who sit across from us, and blushes.

"Well, Matty told me that I could only make one dish, but once I made the salmon, I couldn't stop cooking the filet mignon and the hamburger sliders."

I don't know what to say to Norah.

I look at Matthew, I look at his family and I look at my parents.

They are all enjoying the heavenly delights of Norah's masterpieces.

While they are all smiling and laughing, I feel like I want to cry.

Not out of sadness, but out of happiness.

I meet Norah's amber eyes when I look up.

"Is everything okay?" she whispers across to me.

I nod.

The classical music station is playing a Bach piece in the background.

"I just realized something."

"Really?" Norah smiles. "What did you realize?"

And I tell her, "I realized that I'm going to be okay."

On Sunday I had my last lesson with Dr. Days and Aunt Kilda; and in all honestly, it was the best lesson that I ever had with them.

Today is Monday and the benefit is tomorrow.

Mom and Dad are invited, but they choose not to go.

"Why?" I ask them.

"Because," Mom says. "Tomorrow night is yours."

I guess it makes sense, since after Rose's departure they've been hovering over me again by pressing me to practice sign language with them, handing me my iPod every morning to listen to when I walk with Dad, and begging me to give them a private violin concert.

Lexi calls me and is glad that I changed my mind about the surgery.

"You're coming tomorrow, right?" I remind her about the benefit.

"Yeah, I will. I wouldn't miss it for the world."

The ballroom of the Hotel Del Coronado is transformed into a nightclub.

Two blond girls offer goody bags with the new edition of *Musique Magazine* with Matthew and the Bond Boys on the cover.

There is a gap in the center of the dance floor, and booming music from the playlist that Mel created herself warms up the crowd.

Caterers squeeze through narrow openings on the floor.

Guests buzz straight to the bar like it is a requirement.

Mel, who acts like she is too important to address me, is enclosed within a ring of blond men, (who I assume are the Swedes) and making small talk with them.

"Hey," Lexi turns to me. "You okay?"

"What? Yeah, I'm fine."

I guess I am leaking some emotion onto my face, which Lexi assumes is a sad or anxious look. Although, apparently I'm a walking zombie or moping in her eyes, I didn't realize that I looked so "down" or "odd" until Lexi had picked me up from my house and questioned my look.

"Char," Lexi takes my hand and looks me in the eyes. "It's okay. Just have fun."

A lot of pressure has been on me over the past couple of days. After all, this is my final night of hearing, so maybe I am supposed to look upset.

But that's *not* what I'm feeling.

"Matt!" Lexi turns to wave at the former Lennox band member in the crowd.

Matthew's head spins in our direction and he approaches us wearing a white chiffon shirt, the nicest thing I've seen him wear besides his leather jacket.

As he walks up to us, he pushes Norah in her wheelchair.

"Hey guys," Matthew nods to Lexi and me.

"What up?" Norah waves at us from her wheelchair. "This party looks rad!"

"So, where are the Bond Boys?" Matthew leans forward, bending his elbows on the wheelchair's handles.

"Backstage," I direct Matthew.

"Great," He bends down to Norah's level and whispers a soft "wish me luck" before kissing her on her forehead and walking to the stage.

"Is everything okay, Char?" Norah rolls up closer to me. "You seem . . . sad."

Again with the face! Do I have a sign on my back that reads: "Pity the sad girl?"

"No, I'm just thinking," I say simply.

But I begin to wonder, what is *really* on my mind that is making me give off this weird face?

I leave Lexi to talk to Norah as I make my way to the bathroom.

In case anyone is in the stalls, I turn the water on so it sounds like I'm washing my hands.

Then I just look at myself in the mirror.

All I see is me, dressed in a black blouse with gold beads, lip–gloss, eyeliner and my blond pixie haircut.

What is it that makes me look so sad, so bleak, so . . . concerned?

I push back my bangs.

I'm only five seconds in the bathroom but it feels like I have been here for an eternity.

Then I see it.

I open my electric blue eyes wide now.

I lean forward as close as I can to the mirror, and listen to myself.

40

I walk out of the bathroom and through the crowd of people.

The room has gotten darker and I can hear Mel's voice booming over the mic welcoming Matthew and the Bond Boys on stage.

But I don't stop to look.

I keep on walking.

In a matter of minutes, as I'm slipping my way in between couples, executives and dancers I hear the band crank up the volume, and the room is engulfed by the musical chaos.

I look past the lights and see people dancing, people jumping around, people watching as Matthew and Ron take the microphone and begin to sing.

I wonder if Matthew is looking at me. And if he is, he must be wondering where I am going.

I am listening, but at the same time I'm not listening.

I hear Ron throw his voice to the crowd, drenching everyone in the sound waves that he, Matthew and his band have produced.

The crowd sends out a burst of their own noise and I try to hear Matthew's voice, try to separate that single pitch from the shouts and applause.

In comes the drums and the keyboard, like a bleeding heart, and although I just feel like something implodes inside of me, I head straight for the door.

I am outside.

The Hotel Del is behind me, where I should be. Yet I can still hear Matthew and the band playing in the background. The sound is clear and spirited and makes me think of God.

I still hate you, I laugh silently to myself looking up into the night sky before crossing the street.

The memories of my past and future flash at me like the sudden strumming of a guitar.

I feel like I am complete, that I don't need sound anymore as an excuse to keep me away from tomorrow.

Everything suddenly comes together.

I recognize the street that I am on and before I know it, I'm standing in front of my house.

The porch light is on, and through the window I can see Mom and Dad having some of Norah's leftover hamburger sliders from last night.

Ironically, the kitchen radio is on, playing some famous song that I'm too tired to recognize.

I can feel a smile slide across my face.

I walk up the stairs where I reach for the doorknob and open it.

"Charlotte?" I hear my mom's voice. "Is that you?"

EPILOGUE

I didn't sleep well last night.

I keep thinking back to that night at the Hotel Del with Matthew and the Bond Boys.

I remember walking through the throng of people.

As soon as Mel was welcoming Matthew and the Bond Boys on stage, the room had gotten darker.

But I kept on walking, until I made it home.

Of course my parents were surprised that I had come home early and I explained to them why. Then of course Lexi called me to ask where the hell I was. I sat down and explained the reason for my sudden departure, while in the background I could hear Matthew and the Bond Boys playing.

The next morning was my surgery.

My parents and I didn't say much on the ride to the hospital. I felt that the silence had come sooner, so I turned the radio on.

I heard the strumming of guitars, the smashing of drums, everything that I have listened to over the last month.

I remember the sun shining through the car's window as we drove down the coastline. The sky was blue. The water was blue and the palm trees swayed in the sea breeze.

I remember feeling very sad but sensing a small fragment of happiness buried underneath all those layers of depression and pain, just waiting to come crawling out when the time was right.

It happened in just a minute. We pulled into the parking lot of Coronado Sharps Hospital and I turned off the radio.

I am done writing my letter to Matthew, and I fold it into my pocket just as my parents are escorted into my room by Nurse Frizzy.

I have already changed into the clothes my mom left for me yesterday, and Nurse Frizzy has untethered me from the IV stand. The only fashionable thing that I am wearing is the silky scarlet headscarf that I tied around my semi-bald head.

I am finally free.

I turn to Nurse Frizzy, and sign *Thank you for everything* to her, before I depart from my room.

Dad takes my violin case, as well as my dry erase board as he follows my mom and me down the hallway.

Someone's here to see you, Mom signs to me in her decent sign language as we walk into the elevator.

When the doors slide open, I see the lobby, where two molded plastic chairs reveal two familiar people.

Matthew and Lexi stand up from their seats when they see me.

Instantly, I burst into tears at the sight of them.

Lexi strides up to me and embraces me long and hard until I can barely breathe. She pulls away.

You, she points to me and then pinches her nose. *Smell bad.*

"I know," I say. It's been two weeks since I've taken a real shower.

Matthew is next. He steps forward and gives me a good squeeze of a hug.

It feels good to be around Matthew again, and when I look into his face, he smiles and mouths the words slowly to me, *I missed you.*

"I missed you, too." I say.

Mom and Dad direct me toward the glass doors, where I can see the morning sun rising out over the water.

Standing in front of the doors is Dr. Days in her white doctor's coat.

I stop in front of her.

How are you feeling? she signs to me.

Good, I sign back, and I mean it. I feel really, really good.

I see Dr. Days smile.

She did it. She saved my life.

She claps me on the back, and watches me leave the hospital with my parents and my friends.

I guess my parents had driven both Matthew and Lexi to the hospital because they squish me in the center of the car as Dad drives us to the house.

As we're driving along the coast, Lexi is holding my hand, and I'm resting my head against Matthew's shoulder. My headscarf is tickling the back of his neck by the breeze of the rolled-down window. I reach into the pocket of my jeans and pull out my letter to Matthew.

What's this? I can read his lips.

He unfolds the letter and begins reading it. I already know what it says.

Matthew,

I left because it was over.

I found that what I was waiting to hear was you all along.

You've shared every song that you've written with me, and each was better than the last. You're a good musician, Matthew, and the reason I didn't stay at the benefit was because I have accomplished what I was meant to do.

I listened, and I heard.

That was my mission, and I enjoyed every second of it.

I will miss the sounds, believe me, I will even miss a car alarm going off in the middle of the afternoon. I will miss your voice, Lexi's voice and even my own voice.

But my time was up, and I needed to accept that.

Nevertheless, I won't forget your music.

I will never forget your music.

Here's to new beginnings, Matthew.

Here's to a sound that will never die.

Here's to a new life.

AUTHOR'S NOTE

The idea for this book came unexpectedly: In the summer of 2008, when I was fifteen years old, I was only a kid struggling to put sentences together. My writing has evolved since. First, my grammar was atrocious and my stories were lacking emotion. The problem was that in 2008, I couldn't write a story that carried enough depth and seriousness for anyone who was a young adult to read. I guess you can say that my writing at the age of fifteen was elementary.

But before my family and I went on vacation to Coronado Island, the TV morning news program *Good Morning America* had a story about a woman named Jessica Stone, who—like Charlotte—suffered from type II neurofibromatosis.

Jessica's story was different from anything that I've ever heard. She was diagnosed with neurofibromatosis when she was fifteen and had more than twenty surgeries to remove the benign tumors that grew along her nervous system. She had an estimated eighty tumors throughout her body. They were everywhere, including her chest, throat, spine and ankles. "I'm like, OK, I have this disease that I can't pronounce and I don't really understand it," Jessica told *GMA*. "To me, the diagnosis was pretty much a kick in the gut."

More so, what really hooked me about Jessica's story was the devastating news doctors told her in the winter of 2008. Jessica had already lost the hearing in one ear but then learned from her doctors that a life threatening tumor was lodged on her brain stem. The surgery that would remove the tumor would also leave her deaf. "[I'm] really at a loss for emotions—freaked out actually, to be blunt. Freaked out," she said in a video diary. Jessica was given a month to keep her hearing. To help her cope, she set out with her video camera to record the sounds around her, hoping that one day the images would remind her of the sounds she once loved.

Watching this woman being faced with this unthinkable obstacle was the sole inspiration for *HEAR*. I wanted a character who was just as strong as Jessica Stone, who had the ability to overcome the impossible.

It wasn't that simple, though. I began writing *HEAR* while I was on Coronado Island, and found myself putting my character in an environment where I took the sounds of the waves and the seagulls for granted. I just couldn't imagine a world without sound.

It took me a full year to write the first draft of *HEAR*, and it clocked in at 547 pages. Of course I wasn't surprised when many people turned down the request to read it because it was too long.

I spent the next couple of years editing *HEAR*, by cutting down each chapter to a maximum of six pages or less.

I also started researching neurofibromatosis and was fascinated, yet horrified, at the symptoms of the disease.

I went through revision after revision of the novel, until I had a story which wasn't too long but had the same emotional impact as the first draft.

It had taken me almost four years to finish the final draft of this novel. At one point I had my third draft gathering dust on one of my bookshelves for about a year, before I went back to work on it. By that time it was 2012 and I was nineteen years old. I was mature enough to face this story and take it on as a real writer. Nevertheless, the attention of this story should be drawn toward Jessica Stone, who not only inspired the major plot of this novel but who also inspired me to go on with this story. Despite Jessica's whole ordeal, she still manages to find the strength to focus on the positive.

What made me to write this story based on Jessica Stone's experience is the person that Jessica is. She keeps going through life and admits the hardships of being deaf at one point. "It's really hard being deaf. I wish I would have known this two years ago when we were getting ready for the surgery," she said to a Michigan TV news station in 2011. And although three years ago Jessica made the decision willingly to lose her hearing, she understood that the surgery wouldn't cure her, either. However, Jessica found more reasons to stay positive.

Since her diagnosis, Jessica has wanted to be an inspirational speaker for not only the deaf community but also for others.

Jessica herself is an inspiration for me.

Without her, this novel wouldn't have seen the light of day.

Here's to you, Jessica Stone.

As Matt Nathanson says: *All we are, we are.*

ACKNOWLEDGEMENTS

ac•knowl•edg•ment | ak'nälijmənt |

(also ac•knowl•edge•ment)

noun

The act of expressing or displaying gratitude or appreciation for something.

Let me first start by saying that my gratitude and appreciation for the people who helped guide me to get this sucker published, goes beyond the dictionary definition.

First off, if I don't thank these two important people first in my acknowledgements, I know for a fact that they will disown me. My parents, Michael and Nella Abelson, who have sacrificed everything for me to improve my writing and to find the right people to read and edit this story. Thank you for believing in me during the times when I didn't feel like believing in myself. Your encouragement and wisdom helped me drive this story home.

Second to the woman who saw the potential that this story had and was the one who forced me to see how a writer observes her piece. Jennifer Sarja understood what stories were made out of. Not only did she teach me how to give my story depth and life, but she also taught me what goes on in a reader's head and what they expect to find whenever they pick up a book. And even though I was more than fine with the 547-page first draft of *HEAR*, Sarja proved to me that it was more important to have quality than quantity when it comes to stories.

To my wonderful editor and friend, Sera Sara, who swept me away with her enthusiasm and commitment to get this story finished. Together we drove it all the way from the dirt to the finish line. But the most important thing Sera made clear to me was how a writer's voice changes over time. If it wasn't for her, this story would be infected with my horrendous grammar.

The woman whose opinion changed the way the emotion of this story was played out, Yudi Bennett, pointed out to me the obvious places where I can poke at my readers' emotions. If I wanted my readers to feel something, she told me what places in the story I can take advantage of to extract some sort of feeling. Without her, Charlotte Goode and the rest of the characters in *HEAR* would be less than multi-dimensional.

There's a belief that I have, that if you ever succeed at something with your writing, the most important people you should also thank are your English teachers. Because without them, (let's face it), you would not survive in the real world. I can't thank my wonderful English teacher, Amy Sedivy, enough for taking the time and energy out

of her busy work to read and voice her opinion of this novel. After sitting in her class for four straight years reading everything from Dante Alighieri to Ian McEwan, she understands the writer's mind-set and knows how good stories are told. In addition, I also want to thank her husband, Richard Sedivy, for creating the most eye-catching cover for this novel. For too long, I had always wondered what the cover of my first novel would look like, and thanks to Richard's brilliance and creativity, the dream has finally been fulfilled.

Then there is Lisa Groening, whose strict instructions were to thank her if I ever got published, which only seems fair after all the horrible childish essays that I wrote between seventh and eighth grade. Now, thanks to her, my writing has matured to this, and what a journey it has been.

Deborah Yeseta is my wonderful reading buddy. She encouraged me to read as many books as I can, because she believed that it would improve my writing. And boy, she was more than 100 percent right. It was Deborah who inspired me to keep reading, and I believe that the more I read, the more I began to write better, especially for *HEAR*, so thank you.

And a very special thank you to Elizabeth Slocum who graced this novel with her fine edits.

But the one woman who I should be thanking the most out of anyone is Jessica Stone, the real Charlotte Goode, because this book is based on her. Like Charlotte, Jessica lost both of her auditory nerves to neurofibromatosis but faced her overwhelming challenge with courage and grace. And someone like Jessica who underwent something as unimaginable (a choice between life or sound) should be unquestionably recognized.

Thank you all.

Jacqueline Abelson was born in Pasadena, California, and attends Mount Holyoke College. She is currently working on her second novel.

Made in the USA
San Bernardino, CA
15 September 2013